AUGUST 2018 - ISSUE 143

FICTION

NON-FICTION

Neil Clarke: Publisher/Editor-in-Chief
Sean Wallace: Editor
Kate Baker: Non-Fiction Editor/Podcast Director

Clarkesworld Magazine (ISSN: 1937-7843) • Issue 143 • August 2018

© Clarkesworld Magazine, 2018.
www.clarkesworldmagazine.com

The Veilonaut's Dream
HENRY SZABRANSKI

Sometimes the Discontinuity kinks and curves and flips about as if it is alive.

Openings slide along its vast length like undigested morsels down the gullet of a cosmic serpent. Feathery tendrils shoot out, slowly curling up and fading, each a traveling shadow-slice through some theorized higher-dimensional object. But today . . . today the gap weather is good. There is no sign of movement or instability; the anomaly is razor-straight and steady. A thirty meters high, ten thousand kilometer long, barely visible veil that glimmers on either side of us as far as we can see.

Franco and Zhang float beside me. They are waiting for my command.

"Mads? Are we going through today?"

Franco is impatient. He's very much a get-it-over-with type of guy. Luckily, we've been on enough missions together I feel I can ignore him. But he's right: the idea of turning back dominates my thoughts. It's not too late to stop, to return to the Observatory, though we've signed the contract and the penalty will be high. No doubt Franco and Zhang will denounce my cowardice to mask their own relief—but what do I care about money and reputation anymore?

I check the time since the last change. *One hour twenty-two minutes.* The average is just over seventy-four hours. Information both critical and useless. There's no knowing how long the gap will remain stable. It could be seconds, minutes, days—even months or years. The Discontinuity's size, its shape, the location of the region it opens onto, all of these can and do alter without warning. In the blink of a veilonaut's eye.

"I'd rather be cut," Zhang declares. She's a newbie, fresh arrived from in-system, both terrified and eager. Not a researcher, but one of the new crop of mercenary explorers. When I announced I was going to brave the gap today she had scrambled to tag along. "You may lose a limb or

1

two," she says, "but the v-suit will keep you alive until the medics reach you. There's still a chance of survival."

"They couldn't save Quinn," Franco points out. His tone weary and worldly-wise. He loves to play the grizzled veteran. "Neither the v-suit nor the medics."

Eleven days ago Quinn was caught mid-gap during a change. In some distant lost region of space-time, his missing body parts still tumble. I shudder at the memory.

"But at least he died quickly," Zhang presses on, oblivious to Franco's disapproval. "I'd rather be Quinn than Su. Quinn didn't feel a thing, but Su's still out there, somewhere. Gasping her last air, wishing she were dead. It must be a nightmare."

Franco glares at Zhang. "Not cool, OK? Not the time or place. Not the thing to say."

"Concentrate on what you're doing." My voice sounds perfectly calm over the comms link, with no sign of my irritation at Zhang's ignorant chatter, or the barely contained churn of emotions within me. Perhaps it's the mix of synth-absinthe and sedatives I've dosed up on, their welcome numbing effect. Against mission regs, but the Observatory turns a blind eye, long since drifted from its regimented academic origins. Hardly any exploration would be done, otherwise.

"It's almost time to cross," I remind everyone, careful not slur my words.

Off-comms my breath hitches. Zhang may be crass, but she's not being intentionally malicious. She doesn't know about Su and me; we'd kept it quiet, at first to avoid drama, then as an ongoing game. Not even Franco knows, though he may suspect. And Zhang's right: Su's still out there. Just about now, relative to our timeframe, the last power in her v-suit battery fading. She remains unreachable. Unrescuable. Lost in some distant past or far future. My last words to her before she crossed over had been harsh. We'd argued. I'd called her a fool, a zealot, a selfish dreamer. That she was absolutely wrong about the Discontinuity. I refused to follow her and Quinn on their doomed mission. "I'll find you your world," Su had boasted. "I promise I'll find it for you."

I'd hurled a half-empty drink bulb at her retreating back.

I should have been with her. Been there when the gap swallowed her whole.

That's the other part of the Discontinuity's terror. Crossings are done at speed, to reduce the risk of bisection, which is neat and instantaneous if you're caught passing through mid-change. But even if you're spared that gruesome fate, you can still find yourself stranded on the far side after the gap has moved on. The records show the same region has never appeared twice. Sure, you can survive for a while, protected and preserved in your vacuum suit, but there's no prospect of rescue or return. Cut off forever, unreachable, supplies dwindling, your last desperate pleas will be unheard as the Discontinuity continues to cycle on and the Observatory lights blink away out here beyond Pluto's orbit, their cast-off photons more distant from you than the moment of creation.

To be cut or to be lost. Every veilonaut has to face either possibility each time they pass through the gap.

"You OK, Mads?"

Franco's silhouette floats dark against the veil's Cherenkov shimmer. Just as mine had drifted as I waited, angry and impatient for Su's return, eleven days and only a moment and eternity ago. I was there when the Discontinuity shrugged away a billion suns and spewed forth Quinn's almost-through body. Even now, my hand twitches instinctively, tries to shield me from the memory. Droplets that sparked against my v-suit field like a bloody meteor shower.

"Mads?"

"I'm fine. Let's get into position."

I toggle the nav system controls. Our propulsion backpacks spurt into life, begin a series of pre-programmed maneuvers that will push us closer to the gap.

Zhang crosses herself. She can barely bring herself to look at the rippling veil. Franco, too, is muttering some off-comms incantation. Despite all the known science, the cold hard facts, a fog of superstition still surrounds the anomaly. I don't have much time for the irrational convictions of my fellow veilonauts. More than a handful swear they have glimpsed or felt some mysterious presence as they've passed through the gap. They believe the long dead Others remain inside the rift they created, ghosts trapped within the veil. Some believe the Discontinuity itself is a living, conscious entity, worthy of worship. Even I, normally so scathing of such irrational beliefs, find myself mouthing a silent prayer to the rumored gods of the gap in the moments before crossing. To the angels of the veil, to the ancient long-lost Others. If they exist, or if they don't. *Please protect us as we pass through. Hold the gap open for our safe return.*

So far my prayers have been answered. *Lucky Madeleine,* they call me, *Blessed Lady of the Veil.* A talisman. More successful missions than any other veilonaut.

But I know the truth. The cold, hard math of probability.

3

Everyone is lucky crossing the gap.

Everyone.

Until they're not.

The elapsed time counter ticks over. *One hour twenty-six minutes.*

"Mads? Are you ready?"

One last time, then. One final mission. For love lost, for hopeless hope, for a dream of blue and white and green. "I'm ready, Franco. Are you?"

"Of course."

I take a deep breath, sweat beading on my forehead. "Initiate burn on my mark."

I concentrate on the Discontinuity. For it to do my bidding, just as Su said.

Franco reaches out. Zhang grasps his hand.

"Three."

Zhang stretches towards me, and after a moment's hesitation I take hold of her hand as well.

"Two."

Our breath comes faster, our pulses elevated. We are all linked together, fates entwined. Engine packs perpendicular to the face of the gap.

"One."

I say my silent crossing prayer.

"Mark."

I don't feel anything as I pass through the veil.

Some swear they experience a moment of disorientation. Or, for a few, a full-on rapture. But I've never felt more than a faint tug or seen anything other than a brief blink of blue as I cross over. No visions, no angels.

No ghosts.

No, that's wrong. I *do* feel something. Terror, mostly. Mingled with anticipation. Hope. That more than darkness will greet me.

Hope quickly dashed.

I guess Su was wrong.

Pre-programmed hydrazine bursts from our packs spin us around and decelerate us to a stop relative to the gap through which we've just passed. The Observatory swings back into view, paradoxically only hundreds of meters away and yet at the same time now countless billions of lightyears distant. Our sun still gleams, glimpsed back through the rift, the brightest star even here.

The far side is almost always disappointing. Most of the universe is empty and if the region the Discontinuity opens onto is truly random, then almost inevitably the gap opens onto rarefied intergalactic space far distant from any stars and planets and other forms of baryonic matter. Most often the far side's temperature is barely above the CMB. It's cold, dark, empty; void and devoid.

So it is again, this time.

"OK team." The fact is nowadays veilonauts are paid by the second, not on their opinion of the far side's interest. "You know the drill. We've contracted for at least ten minutes. Timer starts . . . now."

I give the orders automatically, autonomically, trying not to show my relief at surviving transit. Just one more crossing—back to the Observatory—and then I'm done with the Discontinuity and its cruel game of chance forever.

Franco and Zhang deploy their latest research equipment. It's a waste of time, but it's what they're paid to do. Perhaps there's been some breakthrough in observational technology by their sponsors, perhaps this time it'll be different. I'm not holding my breath. Countless automated probes have tried to replicate our work. They always fail. Veilonauts pass through the Discontinuity, make observations, return safely—but nothing of the far side is ever recorded. Only images and measurements of our own solar system, of our own galaxy, as if the hugely expensive and sophisticated machines never crossed the gap in the first place. As if the far side does not exist. Scientists and philosophers argue over the reasons, the consequences, the basic reality of the Discontinuity and of reality itself—but it doesn't change the fact that in order to gain information from the far side humans need to cross and return. Not probes or sensors or other disposable equipment.

"It's a haunting," Su had said, a couple of weeks ago, as we lay tangled together in her dorm bed, sweat cooling on our bodies.

"Hmm?"

"The Discontinuity. It's a ghost. Not real at all."

"Seems real enough when we cross."

"That's what I mean." She tipped her face towards me, her expression earnest, drawing me back to full alertness. "Are we ghosts too?"

"Sexy ghosts." I ran my finger over her shoulder, began to tickle her, and the moment was gone. When I mentioned her words the next day she laughed them off, blamed her introspective mood on a stim-down.

But I remember them now, as I float beyond the impossible gap.

One hour thirty one minutes.

Instead of helping Franco and Zhang, I run my unauthorized scan. I know what I will find before I begin but can't help the growing sense of despair as the search radius expands and the negative result stands. There is no sign of Su, or Quinn's lost half, or any of the equipment they had brought across. Of course not: the gap has moved on, as I knew it had, as it always does. But still I feel a stab of loss and disappointment. And yes, anger. That bastard, hope. Sucking me in once again. Merciless giver and ultimate taker.

"There's nothing here." Zhang interrupts and reflects my thoughts. "I have a bad feeling. Let's go back."

Zhang. The two-time veilonaut. Hardly an expert on the Discontinuity and its mysterious ways.

My scan is almost finished. "Four more minutes," I say. "Them's the rules. Keep looking. You might spot something."

After another minute even Franco chimes in. "Mads, this one's a wash. Just another void."

One hour thirty four minutes.

Why can't I let go? Why can't I cut and run? Su is lost. The others are ready. They've given me permission. The comms record will show the contract violation is not my fault. I can retire, return to Earth, Blessed Lady of the Veil no more.

The scanner gives a soft bleep. Red light. Null result.

"Uh . . . guys. Guys."

It is Zhang's tone more than her words that makes an involuntary shiver run down my spine.

"*Guys.*"

There can be only one cause for concern out here. Only one thing we're constantly afraid of. That can explain the growing tinge of hysteria in Zhang's voice.

There is a flood of relief as I spot the faint glimmer of the veil ahead of us. Still straight, still sharp. The gap still there.

Then I see why Zhang has begun to panic.

And I feel the first stirrings of it myself.

"Oh shit," Franco says, quietly.

I ping the net connection, the always open session to the Observatory servers.

Timeout. Total packet loss. Zero signal.

Through the gap, where we had previously seen the Observatory, the sun, the beacons of everything familiar—there is no sign of them. Only darkness.

They are all gone.

"I can't believe it. It's fucking changed. It's *changed!*"

Zhang's wail is painfully loud in my ears. She stares at me accusingly. "You were supposed to be *lucky!*"

Zero hours one minute.

Every veilonaut's nightmare. Even so, there is a protocol. Numb, I follow it automatically.

Approach the gap. Confirm the change. Trigger the distress signal. For all of the good it will do us.

Glimpsed through the flickering blue static of the veil, our new neighbor universe is dark and utterly unfamiliar.

I cycle through the available options. There aren't many, and none of them are good. Not even close to good. Mostly, what I'm thinking is: *you knew this would happen one day, and now it has.*

But there's a difference between believing something *might* happen, or even that something *will* eventually happen . . . and it actually happening.

Big fucking difference.

"At least we know one thing now." Franco's voice is low and subdued. "The Discontinuity continues to exist on the far side."

He's right, although it's not on my hotlist of items to dwell on right now. Some theories hold that the Discontinuity disappears on the far side after a change, that it relocates to the next distant region whilst the near side remains permanently (and mysteriously) tethered around our sun. A whole class of theories have just been disproved. For all the good it does us, or to the theorists who will never find out they're wrong.

Franco drifts closer to the veil, staring into the darkness beyond.

"The other side doesn't look any more appealing." Once again, I'm surprised by the calm in my voice. As if I'm a creature of pure intellect. Madeleine Field Theorist, Scientist; Emotionless Observer. It's just the shock, I know. The fading meds. Something.

Franco pushes his hand, his arm, his face into the veil. Remains half in, half out.

"My God, Mads, what's he doing?" Zhang is aghast.

I say nothing, only watch, wait for the gap to change and for Franco to be sheared apart. It would just be our luck.

He draws back to our side. I release my breath.

"It's another place," he says. "Another void, similar to this one."

"I can see that from here."

Franco turns towards me. His eyes, glimpsed through the haze of his v-suit field, are also a void. More terrifying than the darkness on the other side of the veil.

"We're lost," Zhang says. "We're lost, and there's no way back."

"We need to keep our shit together." I'm angry with them both; they're not helping push back the panic clawing at the back of my own mind. "Conserve energy. Wait for rescue. That's the plan."

"There's not going to be any rescue." Franco's voice is as dead as his eyes.

"We don't know that. This time could be different." My words, my grasped straws, seem hopelessly optimistic, even to me. But what choice do we have? The Discontinuity follows no patterns. Maybe this time it will be different. Who knows? Nobody knows.

Franco cuts comms. He turns away.

I take hold of Zhang. She's trembling. My grip transforms into a hug. I say, "Shhh. It's going to be OK. It'll be OK. I promise."

A lie. We both know it.

Still, a lie worth saying. Especially now.

Our v-suit's fields merge to form a single surface. It's a practical matter, the shared contact. Reduces the overall field area, conserves energy. It'll help eke out more precious time for our miraculous rescue to arrive. That's what I tell myself, as I cling to Zhang's shivering warmth, let the sensation of human contact overwhelm my darker thoughts.

It is not until some minutes later I question Franco's continuing silence, check on his systems status. It isn't like him to spare on the dour comments.

Shit.

Another hammer blow.

He's done more than just silence his comms. He's made his decision.

On whether to linger and wait for an impossible rescue or take action of his own.

To be cut or to be lost? Which would you prefer? And if lost, what would you do? It may only have been minutes since the gap's moved on, but Franco and I have both had years to dwell on the scenarios.

Franco. Always impatient. The very much get-it-over-with type of guy. No trust he, not in that villain hope.

He has powered off his suit field.

His lifeless, fresh-frozen body orbits ours.

Conserve energy. Await rescue.

It's what the handbook, the guide I helped draft years ago, advises.

Eighteen hours thirty one minutes.

"Why did you keep at it?"

"Huh?"

I am half asleep, lost in dreams of loss, of blue and white and green.

Zhang's eyes are closed but she is mumbling. Not fully alert myself, I struggle to understand her. I've set the v-suit oxygen levels as low as they will go. Everything that can be turned down has been turned down. I've even raided our rudimentary medpacks for their stash of opioid sedatives. They're meant for emergency short-term pain relief, to help take the edge off traumatic injury, but they serve just as well to slow down our metabolism. Anything, everything, to eke out every second of life, every last gasp of vital oxygen. Rescue could appear at any moment, after all, so the more we can draw out our existence the better. Slim or illusory, it's the only hope we have.

"Crossing over," Zhang mumbles. "Why keep doing it?"

"The money, of course." I have no desire to answer with anything as complex as the truth.

"That's not true. It's why *I* do it, sure. My daughter's ill. I need the money . . . to pay for her care. It's the only way I can get it quickly enough." For a moment Zhang's previously placid expression crumples. She's going to cry again.

I didn't even know she had a kid. I hardly know anything about her. There are few secrets amongst the tightly-knit veilonaut community, but I've become increasingly withdrawn from it, retreated into my own bubble. Only Su had managed to penetrate it.

"But you're already rich. Thirty missions-worth. Crazy rich, more than any of us. Why carry on?"

"I don't know."

A long pause. We drift in a dopamine haze. Zhang's breath is slow and steady and warm against my neck.

"They say it's because of Maddy's World. You always coming back, looking for it. Did you see it, really?"

"Shhh." I stroke her short dark hair with fingers that feel distant, balloon-like. "Sleep now. Save oxygen. Rescue's coming."

She mumbles some more but I can't make out the words. Eventually, apart from the gentle sound of her breath, she is silent again.

Maddy's World. A name I've heard all too often.

Again, she's right.

It's why I kept crossing over, again and again. Long after I should have stopped, returned to Earth, humbled and defeated. Trying to recapture that hazy, crazy dream of blue and white and green.

I should have known better.

No darkling void on my first-ever crossing, all those years ago. No mere distant star shining super-bright, a competitor to Sol, or a glimmering nebula, a brilliant globular cluster. No. For me the Discontinuity laid on a real show.

An entrapment.

9

Professors Evelyn Ahn and David Helford—my mentors, my colleagues, my friends—accompanied me. Together we had traveled many months from Earth, studied the Discontinuity from afar and then later at the Observatory, itched to go through and experience first-hand the subject of our research. Finally, the opportunity to leave theory behind and become veilonauts ourselves.

A crescent of blue and white and green greeted us, a sight so unexpected, so astonishing and wondrous we stayed too long, gaping breathlessly, the professors just as awestruck as I. We tried desperately to absorb as much as we could before we returned to the Observatory before the Discontinuity moved on.

A cruel introduction, that first mission. Evelyn and Dave were swallowed by the gap seconds after I came back through. I, the sole survivor.

Officially it's known as Ahn-Helford's World, but that hasn't stopped Maddy's World from being used by the other veilonauts and the journos who still write occasional articles about it. The name that history will record, despite my protests. Yes, Maddy's World. Never glimpsed again, not in all the missions since. Only cosmic darkness and voids, again and again, on each and every trip beyond the cursed veil. It doesn't even rank as a discovery, technically. No corroborating witnesses. Only my word.

Maddy's World. Always with the question, the lingering doubt, growing after each failed mission. A figment of the lone survivor's imagination, a delusion. Or worse: a lie to garner attention, a reputation.

Mad Woman's World. Yes, I have heard it called that. And to my face.

How much worse the doubts would be if the entire details of my debrief were made public, the classified parts the Observatory review panel had deemed too sensational, too surreal, too subjective to allow entry in the record. That even I could hardly bring myself to believe.

Because we saw more than just the gleam of sunshine on liquid water, or the swirling clouds of an oxygen-based atmosphere. A gleaming ring arced over the far side world. A glitter of interlinked rock and ice and metal and glass. With darting motes between the orbiting nodes and delicate elevator spokes threading down to the surface. On the side turned from the golden G-class sun, an unmistakable tracery of nighttime lights: circles within circles, a maze of geometric canals.

Life. Advanced civilization. Perhaps even a glimpse back in distant time to the Other homeworld. Or a colony outpost strung like a pearl upon the Discontinuity's irregular path. Or a mirage. An oxygen-starved, crossing-bedazzled veilonaut's dream.

A dream discovery.

Perhaps only the dream of a discovery.

Su believed in Maddy's World. And Quinn, crazy, doped-out Quinn. He was even worse.

They both believed in the ghosts, the ones supposed to haunt the veil; the living Others, the gods of the gap. Everything. All the stories, all the supernatural guff, every irrational belief I had encountered amongst the Observatory's various communities. Stories I had long since debunked or discarded.

"We can direct the Discontinuity, Mads. It's why the Others made it."

Su floats opposite me in our little dorm cubicle. I suck greedily on a squeeze bulb of synth-absinthe, impatient for its promise of green oblivion.

"Nonsense."

"It's meant to be used. To travel, to reach a destination. Otherwise why was it created?"

"Have you ever considered it may just be a natural phenomenon? That the far locations are chosen purely at random? Don't you think we'd have detected some pattern by now if there were any sort of organization or intent behind it all?"

Even at the time I realized my voice was climbing louder, in frustration, in anger. But I couldn't stop myself: how could she be so . . . so unscientific? So *ignorant*? Despite all her attractions, this one aspect of her, this stubborn streak of irrationality, infuriated me.

"There *is* a pattern," she continued. "You said so yourself: it's clear in Quinn's data. The more people cross, the more often, the greater the likelihood of the gap shifting. The probes and the machines passing through make no difference, but we do. We trigger the change. The gap senses people. It feels us."

"The statistical significance—"

"We *can* control it, Mads. We just need to linger in the veil."

The suggestion horrified me. "You'll be cut or lost. Or worse. There's good reason we speed through the gap . . . "

"Fear!" Su's voice is raised loud as mine now. "We speed through because of fear and habit. But next mission we'll stay in the veil. We'll prove we're right. We'll find Maddy's World again. You and me."

"No." My voice is flat.

She must have sensed my denial, my determination at last. "Fine. It'll be me and Quinn, then. We'll find it without you."

"We? You and Quinn? You know he spends all his contract money between missions getting stoned out of his mind. His brain is mush."

Since when had he become part of "we" ... and when had I become "you"?

And since when had I become this jealous, antagonistic person?

I wanted to reach out, apologize. Despite our differences, Su had been good for and to me, touched places I thought were shriveled, or never existed. Perhaps it was time I recognized how ... significant she was to me.

But she had turned her back. She was gone.

I cursed and threw my half-empty drink bulb at the closing door.

Air is running out.

The suit can tell me exactly how long we have left, but what's the point? The glowing figures are blurred. I can feel the oxygen fading in my lungs, more accurate and more sensitive than any machine. A fatal drowsiness beckons.

There's a ripple upon my retina. The veil shifts again. A barren place, once again a void, one of the countless many that fill and grow in the universe. Barely a glimmer of nuclear combustion from the distantly glimpsed ribbons of matter.

I blink and it changes again.

Filled with a sudden curiosity I expend valuable fuel moving closer to the veil.

It ripples and shifts, strange patterns I've never seen before. Or perhaps not noticed. The veil has always been a thing to be avoided, to be crossed at speed. The risk of being cut, of its boundary shivering and engulfing you accidentally, stranding you on the other side, always a danger deterring close inspection.

But we're going to die now anyway. Past the point of no return. The time for rescue to arrive has run out.

"Zhang."

She is drowsy, barely conscious.

"Zhang. Listen. We have to make it change. It's the only thing we can do."

She shakes her head but makes no other protest as I program our v-suits to cross through.

The gap weather remains good. The veil's faint shimmer a flat curtain. I run my palm through its soft Hawking radiation, poke first a finger, then my hand through.

I still feel nothing.

Does the Discontinuity open onto some hugely distant area of our own universe or onto another one entirely? A brane floating adjacent

12

to ours in the bulk, or another bubble condensed from the chaos of eternal inflation? We don't know. Objects and people pass through freely, without their fundamental constituents flying apart or being annihilated by their antiparticles. Perhaps we've just been lucky so far.

We cross. A shimmer of blue followed by darkness. We cross back. Then over again. And again. Azure stars. Cerulean nebulae. Each time my brow furrows with effort, with concentration. I'm seeking a destination, not just darkness. An end point. With all my heart. With all my soul. That same yearning when I had crossed over the very first time, without fear. No fear. No fear this time. Fear serves only to distract, lose concentration. Fear will quarter me like it quartered Quinn.

"Mads. Mads, what're you doing?"

I am not sure whether it's Zhang's drowsy voice or mine. I don't look at the numbers warning me how far and how fast the fuel level is dropping.

Cross over, back and again, over and over, as the oxygen levels plummet. Lingering in the veil, seeking and plucking its cosmic string, playing it like an instrument. A vast device, a portal gifted to us by the Others, what else could it be? Whorls and stars darting blue. I have always been so fast through, now I begin to see whole vistas I've been blind to before. How beautiful they are. Is this what the other veilonauts meant, how the veil made them feel?

An energy building, an electric crackling tension. Motes of light, star clusters, swirling arms of dust and heat. I can't tell and it doesn't really matter whether they're within the veil or without. Zhang and I are wrapped inside a ribbon of power and light extending from the bright beginning to the inevitable end, and we are traveling along it, forward and back, both at the same moment.

On one side, a change: stars reconfigured, brighter; blue warmth, then back to the other again; a change, two stars, one blue, one red, dancing together . . . my mind concentrated. On a destination. A particular destination in mind. Only that. Only there.

"It's beautiful," Zhang murmurs, her arms tightening around me. Reflected in her eyes: a growing arc of blue and white and green.

A sun golden yellow, hot. I turn to feel the warmth of its radiance, even through the failing shield of our shared v-suit. This sky is not black or star-filled. It's blue.

There's no reason the Discontinuity need open only onto cold dark vacuum.

The tug of gravity, of a world entire, pulls us towards the gap, to our inevitable destination.

A horizon. Beyond the blue shimmer. Rushing towards us.

There is someone there, a silhouette figure. Strange yet familiar. Running. Waving. In welcome or farewell.

The gap opens as I close my eyes.

And say my final crossing prayer.

ABOUT THE AUTHOR

Henry Szabranski was born in Birmingham, UK, and studied Astronomy & Astrophysics at Newcastle upon Tyne University, graduating with a degree in Theoretical Physics. His fiction has appeared in *Beneath Ceaseless Skies, Daily Science Fiction, Diabolical Plots, Kaleidotrope* and *Fantasy For Good: A Charitable Anthology,* among other places. He lives in Buckinghamshire with his wife and two young sons.

The Anchorite Wakes

R.S.A. GARCIA

Sister Nadine's first true thought is of beauty.

Father Paul is delivering a sermon on sacrifice in his deep voice, pausing for emphasis every so often, when the bird lands on the ledge of her squint with a silent flutter of wings. It's smaller than her hand and has the same wavy translucence as the glass in the window across from the altar, opposite her little anchorhold. It tilts its head toward her, and she sees beneath the grayish tinge of its outline, the glowing flow of life within its veins, the pulsing beat of its miniscule heart flashing like a tiny gem.

Beautiful, she thinks. It is beautiful.

And wonders why she thinks this.

The bird hops from one slender foot to another, and for a moment light from the window to her cell that faces the street streams through it. Father Paul's voice fades and she stares as the bird's heart turns into a kaleidoscope of colors. A starburst of energy. Then it leaps into the air and flies above the bent heads of the congregation.

She follows its flight until it swoops down onto the shoulder of a small, dark-skinned girl, her thick hair braided into two plaits that skim a short blue jacket, which matches her worn cotton dress. The bird rests for only a second before darting in front of the girl's face. Her head is bowed, but she opens her mouth and light flashes as it slips inside. Sister Nadine watches as the palest spark slips down the girl's throat and disappears.

The child looks up, looks directly at Sister Nadine as everyone rises to their feet for the hymn. Her right cheek has a dark smudge on it. A bruise.

Nadine wonders how it got there.

• • •

Sometimes, when Father Paul is ministering to the sick, Sister Nadine leaves her cell to pray at the altar. She is kneeling there when the softest sound comes from the pews behind her and pulls her from her prayers.

It is the little girl. She recognizes her now. Louisa Simmons. Last child and only daughter of Merle and Brian Simmons. Merle takes in washing and Brian travels the countryside selling household goods like enamel bowls and cheap bedsheets, cocoyea brooms and doormats. They have five other children, all boys, all perfectly normal and uninteresting.

Louisa is interesting.

She swings her legs as she watches Nadine rise from the ground and come toward her. She does not drop her eyes out of respect, as most of the townspeople do when Sister Nadine comes into the church. She must know Father Paul is out visiting, and she will not be chastised for being in this holy place with her shoulders exposed by the thin straps of her everyday dress. It's pink and more faded than her blue church dress. It exposes a dark blotch of a bruise on her right shoulder.

Nadine sits on one end of the bench and turns her knees toward the girl. Louisa shifts to face her too, head tilted at a strangely familiar angle. Her neat braids sway against her smooth skin, though they are not as long as Nadine's.

Beautiful, Nadine thinks.

"How come you're outside, Sister Nadine?" Louisa asks.

"I'm praying," she says.

"But you pray in your cell. Everyone comes there to ask you for advice."

"You can pray anywhere. It doesn't matter where you are. Your prayers will be heard."

Louisa digests this, her thin legs swinging rhythmically. There is a scar on her left knee.

Nadine looks at the bruise on her Louisa's shoulder and an unsettling feeling tremors through her, as though a hot needle is pressed to her forehead. It is gone before she can grasp it.

"So, you get tired of your cell?"

Nadine nods. Speaking is tiresome for her. It pulls her painfully from her fasting and prayers, from her hymns and spiritual introspection. But she is the anchoress of the church of St. Nicholas and it is her duty to speak with any who seek her wisdom.

"I get tired too." Louisa bows her head, concentrates on her dusty bare feet. "I get tired of my house."

Nadine lets her gaze rest on the wooden altar, polished to a caramel glow by one of the best woodworkers in the parish. On it stands the golden circle of their faith, symbol of rebirth and resurrection. It is comforting, thinking of those that will come and go, and come again. Of the unstoppable flow of life and the immutable glow of the divinity it springs from.

The girl has said something. Nadine turns her head and waits for her to repeat it.

"You can't leave the church either, can you?"

Nadine contemplates this. "I became an anchoress so I would not have to. It is my wish to remain here, to demonstrate my devotion to our faith, and to remove me from the distractions of the world, so that I may come into enlightenment and spiritual wisdom."

Louisa's dark eyes do not blink. "No, I mean you can't leave, even if you want to."

Nadine frowns. "Why would you think that?"

Louisa points to her thick long braids. "I can see your chains."

A tiger came to the church once.

Susanna had brought her middle child, Dennis, to see Sister Nadine because she was at her wits end with him. The tiger, a striped, white beast with metal teeth that glittered like knives, padded up and down the aisle of the church behind them as they knelt to speak to her through the squint. Dennis, a short, round boy with a naughty side, and skin the same hue as the altar, would not meet her eyes while his mother spoke.

"What am I to do with him, Sister Nadine?" Susanna wailed. She ran the biggest food stall at the market and made the best cowheel soup for miles. Dennis was her only child. Children without siblings were often interesting. Nadine did not yet know why this was so.

"Every time he has a nightmare, I don't know what to expect. I'm afraid to sleep most nights. Glen keeps a cutlass by the bed now, just in case."

Nadine thought this over, then spoke directly to Dennis.

"Child, what do you fear?"

Dennis shrugged and slid a sideways glance at his mother.

"Look at me," she commanded softly.

Dennis looked at her. His eyes were not the usual dark brown. Instead they were a pale green, like the sea that bordered St. Nicholas.

"What do you fear?"

"The . . . the dark."

Nadine glanced at Susanna. She had a crease between her brows and her mouth was open slightly.

"You never told me that."

Dennis mumbled, "You never asked."

Nadine made some suggestions and they left, the tiger following them on padded feet. She did not see it again.

She did see Dennis one more time. Harvest Day had ended, and she was looking out of her street-facing window, humming a hymn and watching as people drifted by on their way home. The wind was strong enough to slide beneath her heavy hair and it smelled of the salt sea and the spicy remnants of the curried meats Susanna sold at her stall all day.

Someone waved to her from below the churchyard, down on the street itself. The moon was not out, but she saw Dennis by the light of the tiny golden fireflies that swarmed around him. She watched as he continued on, his parents strolling arm in arm in front of him.

Susanna never mentioned Dennis again. No one did.

Sometimes the spider in her cell spoke to her. It was a curious thing, black as pitch with many more legs than eight. They clicked against the stone and reverberated in the base of her skull. Its eyes were red dots as it sat in the middle of a tangled golden web. The web disappeared into the shadows, finer than hair and twisted into ropes of all sizes, some thick as her finger. Every strand grew from the furred belly of the spider.

"Anchorite Nadine," it would whisper in the voice of her long-dead sister. "Anchorite Nadine. Have you anything interesting to report?"

She had no memory of her answers until the first time after she saw beauty.

"No," she said softly. "Nothing interesting."

The spider pulled on its web, clicking its legs against the stone, and its eyes watched her as she swayed on her knees, hands clasped together, singing.

There is beauty here too, Nadine thought. Divinity in the web that surrounded the spider. In the lyrical whispers that shivered through her skin. In the trance she entered as she prayed. But it's faded and small as the spider. Far away and thin as smoke. It's not as interesting as the beauty she's found in St. Nicholas.

Sister Nadine's second true thought is of warmth.

Merle Simmons passes a bread to her through the window that faces the pews. It is wrapped in a white cloth embossed with a circle of gold and feels like the sun filtering through the cell onto her back. Long after, she will remember the cool smoothness of the wax candles Merle hands her as well.

Louisa is with her, as usual. She sits in the pew behind her mother, waiting and watching, thin legs swinging. She smiles at Nadine, and the skin on Nadine's face stretches as she smiles back, though she does not quite understand why she does this.

"Blessings, Sister Nadine," Merle says. She once sang in the choir and has a voice more beautiful than Nadine's favorite sister. It occurs to Nadine she no longer sings to herself as she carries washing from house to house.

There is the merest shadow of a bruise on the back of the hand that gave Nadine the candles. Nadine catches her fingers as she tries to pull her hand back through the window. They are warm. Warm as the life-giving bread.

"Blessings, Merle." Nadine stares into her soft, dark eyes, but Merle drops her gaze. "Do you seek wisdom today?"

Louisa stops swinging her legs.

Silence shivers through the empty church. Father Paul is in the vestry, writing Sunday's sermon. Nadine can hear the scratching of his pen.

"Just. Just prayers, Sister Nadine." Merle turns her head to the side. "Pray for me and the children."

Sister Nadine feels the hot needle in her stomach this time, and for longer.

"If that is what you wish." She releases Merle's hand.

Louisa stares at Sister Nadine over her shoulder as her mother takes her hand and walks away. Her gaze is strange. Knowing. There is the slightest glow to her; a spark centered above her head. Nadine cannot quite see its shape, but she knows it is important. New.

The Charles boy is an interesting problem. Nadine picked him out the instant she first saw him, as an infant getting water dripped on his head at baptism. Few are quite so present to her. His waving arms and legs were sharp in her vision that first time. She stopped praying to admire the contrast of the pure white of his baptismal clothing against his night dark skin.

Now, he strides through St. Nicholas, the town's resident sagaboy, the gold buttons glittering on his khaki Sergeant's uniform. All the girls would bunch together as he went by and hail him out so they can see the easy smile and flash of white teeth. His hazel eyes trapped a dozen hearts, but he only searches for one amongst the crowd. His steps slow as he passes the town library, every time.

There's a familiarity to him. Nadine has seen the same slow pace before, at night, when she looked out at the stars. Stars that were blocked out by two impossibly long legs strolling across the churchyard, stepping over the tall wrought-iron fence as a human does an ant. Vibrations tremored up from the floor where she knelt, straight to the top of her head. The legs were shiny—glittering hard edges under the moonlight. Multicolored lights cast shadows on the ground as they drew closer to her anchorhold. At first, she could see nothing above them, but then her tiny window was filled with a large eye. There was the faintest whirring as the pupil expanded and contracted, a dark hole in a silver pool that focused on her.

She raised her hands in supplication and began to sing softly.

The colossus listened for a while. Then her window was suddenly empty, and the night sky twinkled at her. I have a secret, the stars said. You can tell no one.

She doesn't. Not for a long time.

Sister Nadine's third true thought is of sweetness, and it slips beneath her skin and makes a home.

Louisa is alone today and she has a small slice of sweetbread wrapped in a paper napkin. She holds it up to Nadine's squint. Services are over for the day, but Nadine has not closed the shutters. It's the wrong window to come to, but before Nadine can chide her, Louisa speaks.

"Blessings, Sister Nadine. I've come for wisdom."

Nadine accepts the sweetbread. The green, red and yellow of the preserved fruits embedded in it catch her eye like jewels.

"Please eat it. Susanna made it special for Harvest Day today. I bought the first slice."

Nadine studies her through the squint. Her little face is shiny from perspiration and her tiny spark blinks above her head, on, off, on, off. The bruise around her eye is the angry purple of an eggplant.

"Please. Just a taste."

Nadine looks down at the sweetbread. The fruits wink at her, on, off, on, off. She takes a bite.

Sweetness floods her mouth. An earthiness anchors it. Textures chase each other as she chews. Soft, jellied, sweet. The crunch of sugar granules baked into the crust. Her head feels warm and light sparkles in her vision as she looks up at Louisa.

"He won't stop," Louisa whispers, words tumbling over each other. "I know it. He hates us. Hates this place. I'm strong, he won't break me. But my brothers. My mother. Please help us, Sister Nadine. I know you can. I've seen your chains. I remember Dennis."

The name causes a curious blooming feeling in her chest. Fire stretches fingers down from the crown of her head to the tips of her limbs.

"Please pray for us," Louisa says, her dark eyes glimmering with tears. "Pray for real this time. It's Harvest Day. Pray for real."

Nadine's thoughts feel slow. Muddled with sweetness and warmth, her vision speckled with beautiful lights that flicker past in rapidly changing shapes. They are familiar and new at the same time.

"You wish for prayers," she asks, her voice fading in her ears, falling down a deep, dark hole, echoing as it goes.

"Yes, Sister Nadine."

Louisa reaches through the squint and closes her small fingers around Nadine's. Her palms are cotton-soft and they warm Nadine's cold hands.

"Help us. Please help us."

Louisa is right. It is Harvest Day. She can help.

Merle Simmons is in church the next Sunday, this time with all her children. The bruises on her body fade and new ones do not replace them. By Christmas, she's singing in the village parang group and back in the church choir. Louisa joins her there.

No one speaks of Brian Simmons again.

Sister Nadine's mind drifted.

She was distracted by the sparkles in her vision, the sensations of her own body. The wind was hot, then cold. The floor was harder on her knees than she remembered. Food was sublime. She cannot imagine why she didn't notice before. Her heavy robe weighed on her skin, and some days, the heat made her cast it off. She gazed out of her window more than she prayed or fasted. She hummed her hymns instead of singing them. She returned smiles when parishioners blessed her with them.

Everything was so very, very interesting.

The spider in her cell was silent. She watched it out of the corner of her eye, and now and then the strands of its web vibrated—golden flashes of shimmering light. The red eyes grew brighter. The clicking of its black legs louder.

Louisa waved every time she went past Nadine's anchorhold.

Sometimes she carried books to her library, or escorted children to and from the school. Other times, she was arm in arm with Joshua Charles, his fine buttons shining, his smile only for her. It wasn't hard to see why. Louisa's brown eyes were bright as the spark above her, her hair a springy black cloud around a perfectly oval face. Her lips were the palest pink and her curves generous and rounded. Her laughter was as infectious as her love of learning. She carried joy in her and shared it with everyone she met.

Nadine waved back every time.

One day, Nadine finished her prayers and opened her eyes. The spider stood before her, furred black legs silent on the stone floor. She breathed in cold, foul air that was recycled many times. Around her, strange sounds echoed. The whirs and clicks and hammering of machines. The murmuring of many voices. Her vision resolved as the sparkles finally faded from it, and she could pick out the voices of hundreds of her sisters, far, far away.

Home, she thought. But not really. Not anymore.

"Anchorite Nadine," the spider said in a voice like silken steel. Golden showers of swiftly cycling code spilled between its mandibles and spread outward from the Hub beneath it in countless threads, linking Anchorite after Anchorite on world after world.

It is Harvest Day.

"Anchorite Nadine."

She knew this in her tiny cell on St. Nicholas, where an infinitesimal bit of her code remained, sealed off by new code born some time ago, on a day when she first glimpsed the beauty of an innocent soul.

This bit of her intelligence remembered other things too. Tigers that couldn't be seen by others. Missing people—children who were always forgotten. Colossal machines that strode the world. All of them born of nightmares and fears and the manipulation of synth-matter and code.

Most of all, she remembered the violence of a man toward his daughter, toward his family. A miniscule part of the violence that lurked in the cold, vast universe, where war raged endlessly while anchorites hid the most gifted of humanity and waited for them to mature into something interesting . . . useful. To grow fear and pain into weapons that could win an endless war. A war begun for reasons no one remembered. A war that gained new fighters with every Harvest Day.

"Have you anything interesting to report?"

Missulena's red eyes burned as it clicked its legs and waited. In them, she could see the ever-changing code of the WarSong, created by the quantum AIs of Terra to better direct the conflict toward its unknowable end.

There is no end.

It was her fourth true thought, and after it, there were no more thoughts that belonged to the Hub and Missulena. No more code prayers that fed the most interesting things in St. Nicholas into the Hub and back to the WarSong AIs.

Violence begets violence and every Harvest delivers more death to the Harvested. To other worlds. To a humanity that knows nothing of the WarSong and its never-ending search for new weapons. For new Users.

A humanity that did not ask for this.

There were no more lies in her code.

"No." Sister Nadine hummed her hymn in reply. "There is nothing interesting to report."

Missulena thought on this. "What of the colossus builder?"

"Lost to an accident last summer." Nadine effortlessly built code to confirm this, swaying on her knees and praying it into being in her anchorhold.

The rest of her raised her hands to Missulena and sent out WarSong hymns, as expected.

Missulena expanded and contracted, as if it took a deep breath. "Unfortunate. St. Nicholas has given us much. Atom eaters. Ground shakers. Perhaps next Harvest."

"Perhaps," Nadine agreed.

In St. Nicholas, she prayed new code that sparkled with soft translucence and sank into the golden skeins that touched her from Missulena's web. The Hub absorbed them while Missulena directed a ceaseless chorus of hymns and attended to prayers across her Anchorite networks.

"Blessings, Sister Nadine."

She sang Blessings back to Missulena and watched her song travel the Hub to her many sisters.

Warmth caresses her hands while cool salt air wafts around her. Her body is heavy with exhaustion and exhilaration. Slivers of stone stab her knees through the cloth of her robe. Her mouth tastes of dry sweetness.

Sister Nadine opens her eyes and sees Louisa's smiling face. Her fingers tingle in Louisa's grasp.

"Blessings, Sister Nadine," Louisa says and tears slip from her eyes. "Many, many blessings."

It takes some time for Nadine to gather her own thoughts. It's harder to be clear now her words are her own.

"How did you know?" she asks. Her voice sounds harsh to her own ears, rusty with disuse.

"I saw your chains. Remember?"

Nadine looks down. Her braids glimmer against her brown robe, yellow ropes of code that snake down from her head, under the door to her anchorhold, out to the altar and the glowing circle of her amplifier that stands on it.

"Not chains," she says. "Code."

Louisa laughs and nods. "Yes, Sister. Code. I could see it from the time I was small. It was everywhere. In the walls, in the earth. It all led back here. To you. But I wasn't sure what it meant. Not until Father's harvest."

Nadine stands. Several of her braids link her wrists to Louisa's as she, too, rises to her feet.

One braid links to the spark above Louisa's head, making it the crown jewel in a shimmering, translucent halo. Nadine catches a breath looking at it, and a *feeling* blooms in her chest, tightens her throat.

"Coder. You are a Coder."

"Is that what you call me?" Louisa tilts her head and winks. "I thought I was crazy for the longest time. I could see so many strange things. Remember people everyone seemed to forget. But then I spoke to you and I knew you saw the same things. Remembered what I did. I knew I wasn't alone. That I could trust you."

She squeezes Nadine's fingers.

"That you would protect me. Protect us."

"But your father . . . " Nadine struggles to find a way past the uncertainty weighing her tongue. "I Harvested him. His violence made him interesting." Nadine can't tell her all that means, but Louisa knows.

"You did what you had to do," Louisa says touching her forehead to Nadine's. "You protected us.

Nadine pulls back to stare at her halo. There is wetness on her face. She wipes it away. "Coders are rarest of all. But they take you young, so you can be taught WarSong. Once they're done, there's nothing left."

"I think I knew that." Louisa hugs Nadine to her and the anchorite smells the soft florals of talc powder.

Nadine holds her, palms prickling with starchy feel of the cotton dress beneath them. "You were innocent. I could not let you go. I could not let more violence happen to you."

"I'm sorry," Louisa whispers. "There was a bird one day, and I'm not sure how I knew what to do then, but . . . I think I broke your code. Rewrote it a little. I needed someone to help me. I wanted someone to see me. Really see me. And I *felt* it work. I felt a little bit of you go. I erased part of you. I'm sorry."

"I am not sorry." Nadine pulls back. "I heard your Code and it was . . . interesting. I have sung it to my sisters. Some are very far away and may never hear it. Others may find it more interesting than their First Hymn, as I did."

Louisa's eyes widen. "I never imagined . . . how many other worlds are there? How many like St. Nicholas?"

"I cannot know. Some of my sisters anchor worlds so precious, they are not linked to the Missulenas, and there are many Hubs besides mine. But one day, your Hymn may reach them. Perhaps they will like it. Perhaps they will listen."

The door to her anchorhold creaks open. Joshua Charles waits there, a baby girl in his arms. He bounces her against his big shoulder as his gaze falls on Louisa. The baby is wearing her Sunday best, as is Joshua.

It's Harvest Day, Nadine remembers. And this is what Louisa was protecting. This is why it had to happen now.

There is a question in his eyes and he signs to Louisa with one hand, "*Is it done?*"

"Almost." Louisa turns back to Nadine and her halo flashes on, off, on, off. Energy pulses into Nadine, setting her on fire before a cooling rush floods her to the tips of her toes. Her braids waver and shorten. Her links to Louisa fade away. Her mind expands, infinitely clear. The world comes into focus. Her senses run riot with color and sensation. She feels each breath in and out of her chest.

She can sense more than the amplifier that can reach every mind on St. Nicholas. She's no longer chained to the never-ending prayers and hymns of the Hub.

She feels *present*.

"I've updated your Code. You can come with us now. You're not tethered here anymore. Wouldn't you like to see the Harvest? Our Harvest?"

It won't be like the WarSong's Harvest, Nadine knows. It won't be pain and fear and death. It will be love and hope and dreams come true.

It will be like the child in Joshua's arms, glowing with the kaleidoscopic colors of a supernova, chubby palms waving as she stretches toward Nadine.

"Yes," Nadine says, and holds out her arms. Joshua hands the baby to her, a warm bundle that smells sweet and new. Her skin is dark as the night sky, like her father, and spangled with millions of stars shaped like her mother's jewel—her Codestone.

World maker, she thinks.

The baby smiles and pats her face with cotton-soft hands. Sister Nadine smiles back and whispers to her, "Hello, beautiful."

ABOUT THE AUTHOR

R.S.A. Garcia's debut science fiction mystery novel, *Lex Talionis,* received a starred review from Publishers Weekly and the Silver Medal for Best Scifi/Fantasy/Horror Ebook from the Independent Publishers Awards (IPPY 2015). She has published short fiction with *Abyss and Apex, SuperSonic Magazine* (Spain) and the *Apex Book of World SF Volume 5.*

She lives in the Caribbean nation of Trinidad and Tobago with an extended family and far too many dogs.

Kingfisher

ROBERT REED

1

And then there was quite a long time with nothing to chase. No suggestive tracks in the ice, no hopeful stories told by misinformed strangers. The air didn't hold any name glancingly resembling her name, and there weren't even rumors about intriguing places beyond the endless horizon. Without direction, only random motion was possible, and a miserable expanse of empty moments and boredom, and of course he considered stopping. Any sane mind would want to quit. Except he was far more than just another sane mind. No, he was also strong and disciplined, and most important, ridiculously stubborn: these were the attributes that he had always cultivated, and that's why he kept wandering the ice for many more useless centuries.

But even the stubbornness of gods has limits. So when the nothingness didn't end and the urge to be done didn't end, there came that moment when, at last, he paused. Yes, he gave up the chase. The best place among a thousand random places was selected, and he inhabited one patch of ice for a long quiet. This was rest. He was cultivating his energies. That's what he needed most desperately. And since every rest demands shelter, he built a little home that gradually grew larger, but he always lived simply, and what followed was a very long interval when he did quite a lot but always in the same place.

The truth was, doing nothing had happened before. There were seven interludes before this one, according to his count, and each of those intervals had felt permanent. But endless life always invited monotony, and there was always the temptation to fall back on the habit of relentless motion. And that's what happened this time. A passing traveler supplied both a rumor and a name, and the hunter once again boarded his skimmer, setting out across the shifting pack ice, crossing a chain of days and ages, accomplishing nothing besides convincing himself that the chase remained useless and nothing would change. So yes, he stopped once more. Except this interlude felt different. Not only did he build a fine house, the best of the nine, but he also wooed a wife who could share his bed and make conversation, and in the darkness, she sounded just human enough to make him forget Her.

For seventeen centuries and one thousand days, that was his life.

Except nothing had changed, of course. He was a searcher and it was his nature to pursue, and the inevitable found him standing outdoors. Which was or was not an important detail. The incident was so ordinary, so pathetically simple, that there was no point claiming that being indoors would have saved him. No, he simply let himself become careless. Standing on the roof of his fine house, looking across the endless ice, the habit of searching for an emerald skimmer ambushed him. Of course there was nothing to see, certainly no skimmer or any other machine in motion, or even a sound that might be confused for blades biting into the white face of the world. But there was still enough imagination inside his soul to trigger ancient habits. He looked for Her and too many memories woke up, and he couldn't stop them or blunt them, and that's why he dropped to his knees and wept, and then as a distraction, in despair, he chopped off one hand and stared as the hot blood splattered and froze. There was a battle inside him, and it wasn't profound or even a little noble. Just a cluster of fond moments with the only woman who had ever mattered to him. That's what ambushed him, and that's why he was left in such a desperate state.

Stack the moments of this man's life on top of one another, and he was left kneeling and bleeding before a looming, precarious mountain. How could any woman's face or voice or her simple name mean so much after so long?

Yet they did.

If guilt was a liquid, it would be black, and its bitterness was inside his mouth, crawling down his miserable throat. Yet even this ambush of guilt should have done no worse than deliver a few years of gloom. So maybe something else brought him to his feet again. A premonition, a hope. Stupidity, most likely. And standing again, flexing that partially regrown hand, he understood what would happen next and didn't even pretend to resist.

The ninth house was abandoned.

He told the wife everything. Because he was never a creature of secrets and she knew him well enough, he didn't need to explain for long. She had always understood what was probable, and nothing could be earned by fighting him physically or trying to bury these fossil urges with fresh, sordid emotions. No, the wife simply wished him a long voyage ending in disappointment and oblivion, and she avoided using his name, which was another kind of curse. Then he walked to the berth where his skimmer waited, sleeping inside a helium bath, and while the trustworthy machine woke from hibernation, the man did what he always did, facing the chase without direction: He picked up a straight tool and flung it over his back, as hard and far as possible, and then he walked across smooth ice and broken ice to where the tool was waiting. Its straightness offered two directions. That was critical. Infinite choice was reduced to its minimum, and having made his selection, he fueled and provisioned his skimmer, stubbornly ignoring his house or any quasi-face that might show itself.

He was climbing aboard when the wife emerged long enough to repeat one of her curses.

"A long journey and then Death," she said.

But in the end, with surprising tenderness, she spoke his name.

"Kingfisher," she said.

Then he left her and he cried about it, out-and-out sobbed, and three days later, still weeping, Kingfisher came across just enough rumor to begin the chase all over again.

2

The face of this world was nearly infinite, and its skin was ice. The deep waters froze and sharp frost came with every fog and hard deep unpredictable snows would descended where they wanted. Seams and pressure ridges were common features, and bergs standing like mountains. Every portion of the world's face had been shattered. Impacts or wind or upwellings of oxygen might tear apart the whiteness, leaving open water. But those oceans were temporary. The atmosphere was many thousands of kilometers deep, thick to the top, layers held aloft by a sequence of demon roofs. That wondrous, abiding cold always rebuilt the ice and sent more snow falling, and there was always too much ice for the infinite world, and when he did nothing, a man could stand beneath the starless sky, listening to the roar as the ice fought against itself, feeling the tremors passing through his ageless bones.

The chosen direction had to be followed, but Kingfisher's skimmer was too smart to obey simple lines. Artful little swerves let it attack each ridge at an angle, and where possible, the machine opened the jets full, launching its body on long airborne arcs. These were normal tricks, and Kingfisher didn't bother to worry, much less steer. He occupied his mind by scanning for skimmer tracks, and nearly as important, watching for trash or broken machines that might bring a price to the right buyer. Two days of that, and nothing was seen. Then on the third day, shortly after waking, he spied a small ark straddling pontoons. The ark's inhabitants had also seen him, and chattering among themselves, they wondered if that flying man was bound for the city.

"Which city do you mean?" asked Kingfisher, ready to pin a name to his inadequate, forever changing maps.

But arks were usually prickly and self-contained, and this particular example was worse than most. It decided to say nothing, not one mouth speaking until after the interloper had fallen out of sight.

Midday brought a muncher chewing up ice by the megaton, filtering out the salts and metals and rarer elements too. Kingfisher offered polite greetings, and the machine reacted with the question, "What kind of hurry takes you, human?"

"I'm searching for a craft like mine, but larger and swifter," Kingfisher explained. "Lovelier and better piloted too." Then he gave every old tag-number, none of which were likely to be valid anymore.

Giant munchers rarely pay little attention to those things that weren't vanishing into their gaping maws. Knowing nothing about any skimmer, that machine preferred to complain about how the ice was both too thick and too poor. The world's cold was only growing and the treasures from the sky were far too rare anymore. "I am concerned about the future for us all," said the muncher.

"Be concerned for me too," said the human. "Because I don't have time to worry."

Then later on that arbitrary day, just as Kingfisher was thinking about dinner and sleep, he passed close to a blue-sturdy. Like every other ark or machine or indifferent citizen, that creature had no memories of any other human skimmer, much less one woven from emerald and elegance. Through a second-rate translator, using a female voice, the blue-sturdy asked how this human knew that this other vehicle had come this way.

"I had help," Kingfisher said. "A tool I trust pointed me along this line."

Living within a pressure ridge, the creature stole its life energies from rubbing plates of ice. What appeared at the surface was a tiny fraction of the gigantic entity—a ten-kilometer-long forest of heads and temporary limbs and one voice and various machines built to serve many roles, including talking to the human monsters. The blue-sturdy claimed that she had seen everything and everyone that had passed in this darkness for the last twenty thousand years, and no skimmer like that had ever shown itself.

"I am sorry to hear so," Kingfisher allowed. But he intended to press on, loyal to his latest guess.

"And you won't find anything else beyond," the beast added. "Not for another million kilometers, at least."

Blue-sturdies reached deep under the ice, and they had amazing ears. With his little mouth, Kingfisher asked those ears, "Where should I aim?"

"Toward the city, I should think."

"Which city is that?"

What translated as laughter washed over him. "Only the greatest city left in the great endless world, and how can you not know it is here?"

"Because I am an idiot," he said.

Talking down to humans was a blue-sturdy pleasure. And that was the best way to charm them—invite their feelings of superiority.

"I will give you another line to follow," the voice said. Then most of those temporary limbs as well as every flexible machine pointed in an entirely new direction.

"You say this city is near?"

"Not that, no." With considerable precision, the blue-sturdy told Kingfisher how far he would need to travel.

"And there are humans in this city?"

"Many or none. I would have no way to know, if I cared. But maybe you will find some other voice, and it will speak to you, and you will believe what you hear and give up this pursuit."

"Oh, that will not happen."

Kingfisher told his skimmer to turn, and it obeyed in its own fashion.

Then the voice was falling behind him. "How long have you been following this gemstone craft?" asked the blue-sturdy.

Kingfisher told. Or at least he surrendered the best of the various estimates, which happened to be the most extreme.

"I do not believe you." But having dismissed the impossible number, she asked, "And why are you are searching for this other human?"

With force, Kingfisher said, "It is love."

Blue-sturdies had no use for bonding with any creature, particularly their own independent kind. But the human concept was strange enough to earn several days of silent respect. Then as Kingfisher's skimmer left the reach of her transmitter, the alien pointed out the obvious: "But you have the slower craft. According to your own calculations, this is a race you must lose."

"It is mine to lose," he said.

"And even if the city welcomes you, your love will be elsewhere."

"She probably will be."

"You are uncommonly foolish," said the translated voice. "You have missed her before and will miss her again, and where is the good?"

Kingfisher laughed.

"Don't forget," he said. "Humans never grow old."

Sentient life was always immortal. The blue-sturdy's response was decanted into the bluntest of questions, "So what?"

"And this ice, big as it seems, is only so big." Then Kingfisher laughed louder, adding, "Give me a little less than forever, and my love and I will eventually find ourselves inside the same space, inside the perfect moment. I promise it."

3

"The world is simple until you put your nose down close to it."

She had said those words. She. The ageless lady who piloted that lovely emerald skimmer. In this memory, she was holding him by the back of his bare head. He would never forget the amusement in her voice followed by laughter that wasn't amused. She was a powerful creature, though he wasn't certain if she pushed him down or if he had fallen willingly. Either way, his nose was pressed against the frigid ice, and then she said his name.

"Kingfisher."

He loved to hear his name. Always. But particularly from her mouth, the sound of it wrapped happy inside all that history.

"What does the ice show you, Kingfisher?"

She must have been furious with him; that was the only reason to play the bully. And there would have been good and justified reasons for her rage. Though he couldn't manage even weak guesses about what he might have done or not done to deserve this abuse.

"You know what the ice shows me, Kingfisher."

"Trash," he said into the world's face.

She let him go.

But he kept that nose down, and the eyes. "The rubbish that falls and the rubbish that floats up from below," he said.

She said, "No, that's not what I see."

"You see me," he said. "I'm ugly trash lost in the ice."

Exasperated, her anger shifted directions.

That was one of Kingfisher's talents. The woman was a great pilot, but he was the master who knew how to steer the pilot, using nothing but careful phrasing and some play-acting.

"No, you aren't trash," she said.

She said, "What ice is . . . ice is the promise of perfection."

That was an old speech being repeated, or it was brand new to the moment. Kingfisher didn't have enough memory to feel certain either way.

"Done properly, the marriage of cold and hydrogen bonds allows a crystalline purity that doesn't need to end. Ice to the bottom of the sea. Ice to the ends of this body. Ice white under the stars, unbroken and smooth and strong enough to hold onto many worlds, if need be." The great pilot was never sentimental, unless she was. "Now look up at the stars, Kingfisher. Gaze at my sky."

He rolled over and blinked two times. At least in the memory, that's what happened. Two blinks, and he looked.

Then she told her little man, "The sky is complicated until you pull back your nose. And what do you see then?"

"Empty cold beauty."

"Blackness," she corrected. "The perfect opposite of ice, yes."

By itself, none of this made for lasting memories. Not him being flung down, not her lecturing about grand meanings. What happened next was what fixed these moments into the most trustworthy places inside his skull. The woman laid down beside him. She was larger than Kingfisher, and not just a little larger. She had a splendid body and a mind already ancient and well-traveled, and she was wise in more ways than a foolish man could count. And she was naked.

"I want you, Kingfisher."

She had never said those words, or made any sign that she desired him. This was the first time.

"While we rest between perfections, take me," she ordered.

That is what he did.

There were other occasions when they coupled, many times. One hundred and two blisses more, according to his best count. Which might not be an accurate tally, since the eons wore away at even the sharpest memory, and he never had the finest recall. Without question, she was the smarter one.

"I love you."

There were long, long intervals when he spoke to nothing but that one recollection. The cracked and filthy, profoundly imperfect ice stretched towards the false promise of a horizon. The starry sky had been replaced by blackness encircling blotches and wisps of bluish light. His skimmer stole hydrogen from the ice, feeding its reactors, and he stole fuel from the skimmer to synthesize his meals, and there was nothing else to do but watch the past and every imaginary future.

Then came a momentous day when three distinct entities were met, and one of the strangers had genuine news, and that excitement made Kingfisher miss the singular woman more than ever.

"This time will be different," he told himself.

A city floated directly ahead of him, and he knew with absolute certainty that he would eventually find it.

"This time will be different," he repeated.

Except that second time, he barely recognized his own voice, each word sliced apart by the consuming fear that against the miserable odds, he would be right.

4

The city was twenty years and thirty-seven days in the future. Great reaches of ice had to be crossed, delays brought by trash hunting and half-kilometer snows. But tracking the target was easy enough. Cities were slow and massive, and as promised, his quarry was an absolute giant. The ice before it had to be shattered and melted, taken into the reactors and retrofitted stardrives to be used as propellant for the jets. And an open ocean was born in its wake, much of that liberated water close to boiling. But water quickly forgets, and that ocean soon forgot the city, growing chill while every little current played out, the stillness taking hold before the freezing began. That's when Kingfisher was doubly certain that he was on the right course. He came to a plain of pure hard ice, frozen deep and pretty. Sometimes he paused to lay down microphones and listen with their ears. He couldn't hear the city's engines, not like the blue-sturdy could. What he heard and weighed was the music of new water freezing directly ahead of him. Then other tools looked deep into the water, reaching down five hundred kilometers of liquid and various high-pressure species of ice—a sum that was too thin by quite a lot. And he knew what that meant.

His skimmer didn't need to adjust its course. Straight on, as fast as possible, and to make the journey quicker, Kingfisher synthesized drugs that brought sleep for days and days, all of it free of dreams.

Three years to go, and the ice ended. The skimmer reconfigured its hull, sprouting sleek pontoons while its jets made bubbles of gas and roaring noises. But that flat-out racing didn't last long. Waves appeared, peaceful and scattered to begin with, steam rising from the cooling water. Again, Kingfisher stopped to listen, and that's when he heard the powerful stardrive jets thrusting hard and steady. So now he began taking samples of the water, pulling out rare ions and lost nano-trash and those tiny furious organisms that existed only in the sewers of cities and the guts that emptied themselves into a city's sewers.

Human shit was dissolved in the water.

The human wanted to fly the rest of the way, but the skimmer refused. Its AI was too old and stubborn in its own ways, forbidding wings in place of pontoons. In fact, it made itself go slower than necessary, and that caution was met with increasingly rough seas and wild blizzards that would have tossed it from the sky. A pilot can demand courage, but the machine had enough imagination to scare itself. What if there was a big piece of trash floating ahead of them, unseen? Or worse, what if the city's inhabitants were hostile or violent or insane, littering their wake with fusion mines, or worse?

Four months out, and the ocean was a maelstrom that couldn't be avoided. Skimmer and man both tried to steer out of its wake, but the city was so broad and destructive that there was no escaping it. Both of them agreed to give up, retreat, and find new ice and then try to flank the slower target. But as if hearing that threat, the city decided to show itself. The entire horizon was covered with its marvelous light, radiant curtains rising into places that had no stars and very little trash, every possible color abundant and swirled together into one grayish whiteness that pretended to shimmer happily when the man stared at it for too long.

There were days when progress was slow and ugly. The furious ocean wanted to keep them back, and they were sunk ten times every minute. But the gigantic city also reached deep, its jets twenty kilometers below them, and that's why the final week was the easiest of all. Traveling in the slipstream, the scalding water lay calm on the surface, and Kingfisher decided to slow down quite a lot. He wanted the best place to dock. Studying the architecture of alien buildings and the machines flying above and listening to a multitude of languages, only some of which could be translated, he achieved one critical insight. This was not a city. This was a continent—an ancient word brought out of storage and misused—and gazing at that floating wonderland, Kingfisher said to himself, "She must, must be here."

And that's when he gave up searching for the best berth, silencing the skimmer's doubts and turning both of them for shore.

There was no first moment, no word or glance that came before any other, and no happenstance collision between the mismatched bodies of strangers. For Kingfisher, he had always known the woman and they were always accustomed to one another, if not yet lovers. In those earliest memories, he couldn't even recall romantic feelings towards the beauty. Because they seemed to be colleagues. Because she was his ranking superior, and untouchable. Traveling together, they were doing work full of critical details, chasing goals that had long ago escaped his understanding. But their lives must have been vital. How could it be otherwise? There were arks and floating villages where they stopped to rest, to speak to the locals, although that didn't seem to be their normal, official job. Kingfisher remembered very few specifics, except for being certain that he enjoyed being social. And one clear memory involved a young ark that didn't know enough about the world where it had been born.

"What you see is not endless," the giant woman explained to the ark. "But the seemingly endless water and ice that surrounds us . . . all of this is just the tiniest, least important piece of the world."

Arks used to fall from the sky with the trash. They usually came as eggs, totipotent envelopes meant to bring the best of an alien world. Never much bigger than a big skimmer, each contained a complicated stew of instructions and stored genetics and just enough machinery to build a large-enough habitat. Every ark was a complete world sitting inside a bottle, enclosed and eternal. A little drip of power from the outside; that was all they needed. And some of these arks weren't just born ignorant, but they refused to learn anything what was beyond their own diamond wall.

"The Beltrami pseudosphere," the woman said.

Kingfisher must have known those words and what they meant. Except they were only random noise now.

"We are riding on a starship shaped like a Beltrami pseudosphere," the woman said. "The world we know is the ship's bow, round and flat. Our ship began its journey with the helpful shove from an exploding star, and ever since, whatever stands in our way is absorbed. Interstellar hydrogen gas collides with the deep atmosphere and the demon roofs, and then moving slower, it combines with the air's oxygen to make water. To build snow. That falls and becomes the ice, and the ocean grows deeper, and the water that's pressed against the ocean floor is torn apart for its hydrogen, as a fuel, while the liberated oxygen bubbles back up to the air. But helium is different. Helium doesn't play with any element, including itself. The demon roofs slow it, and the gas mixes into our breaths, and then helium scrubbers pull it free with laser light and zero-degree traps. Because helium is a worthy starship fuel too. And so is everything else, by the way. The dust between stars collides with us and is absorbed. Comets and lost machines and clumsy starships and arks that aren't as good as you. Anything with mass that comes into our path is essential to powering the world's single rocket engine."

She was trying to teach the ark to see its extraordinary luck. That was every teacher's job, trying to make the student appreciate what couldn't be seen. And unknown to her, she was also delivering the lecture to the innocent idiot that was Kingfisher today.

"Hyperfiber," she said.

That word he could never forget.

"The pseudosphere is built from hyperfiber. The highest grades, thousands of kilometers thick and pure. And we are barnacles riding the hull."

Whatever "barnacles" meant.

"I am one very important crustacean," she said, "and the remarkable hull hides under this little endless ocean of ours. The hull's mass gives us much of our weight. The ocean gives us a little more. If we drained the ocean, you'd find your bottle resting on a gray plain that is just slightly, so imperceptibly, less than flat. You see, the bow tilts towards its center, and it grows steeper as you move inwards. And if you rolled to the middle, what would you discover? A bottomless hole capped with machines and demon floors and protocols and repair systems. The pseudosphere becomes a magnificent column that perpetually narrows as it reaches far behind us. And all of these machines and demons and systems and rules constantly sort out the captured grit and shit. Helium is squeezed into Bose condensates, and the hydrogen is yanked from the oxygen, then compressed into metal. Every fuel is shoved into that magnificent mouth. Then trickery and crude physics, plus bracelets of degenerate matter, trigger all recipes of fusion.

"A quasar. One narrow and spectacularly tamed quasar, self-contained and relentless. That's what drives us between the stars and beyond the stars. The engine's acceleration is another part of what we feel when we stand and when we sleep. Be aware: Every piece of this ship serves the ship. I am here to do just that. And my Kingfisher too. Ocean and atmosphere are here to slow what falls on us, and to let us do our work more easily. We are generous creatures, let me tell you. Warn you. You exist because of our considerable kindness. Do not forget that. One unkind impulse and the flip of a switch . . . that is all that it would take for this icy watery world of ours to be drained away, roaring down that endless hole, then transformed into the purest fire."

There was a pause, long or brief. Kingfisher could remember the silence either way.

Then the ark asked its only question. A mishmash of dense, interwoven bodies and species and genetics generated a child-human voice that wanted to know, "And who holds this awful switch?"

"I do," said the giant woman. "I am this ship's pilot, and I am your future."

Then she laughed, enjoying some or all of this teaching business.

6

Rules could be ignored, laws subverted, and every code was subject to slow erosions. But a skimmer owned by a human was always secure from theft or abuse, and the way it had always been was the only way it could be.

Kingfisher found and claimed an empty berth.

"Boundless storage," he wanted.

These docklands were owned and managed by an AI with one thousand bodies and some very clear ideas about the value of its services. "One sum for every three point nine days in cold storage."

"No," the human said.

"Leave and find better," the machine suggested.

Find better first, then leave. That's what Kingfisher attempted, but every other facility was more expensive or offered inferior services.

"Very well," he agreed.

Contracts were etched in digital realms and on the skimmer's belly. If nothing changed, his existing funds would be drained before the next century. Watching liquid helium pour over his old friend, Kingfisher asked about the city's name.

"It has no name but the City," he was told.

So the full name was forgotten or left behind. Then he asked the AI about a skimmer rather like his, but different.

"Never here," the machine answered.

"Anywhere else?"

"A thousand sums for my Citywide inquiries," it said.

"Fifty and my universal praise of your skills," he said.

They settled for two hundred and no praise. Then after a lengthy search—so long that Kingfisher had time to fill a sack with trinkets that might be sold, then walk to the edge of the docklands—the machine reached out to say, "Emerald and with two of the proper codes, yes."

"Where is it?"

"On the other side of the City, before. But it has vanished from its berth."

"She left," he said.

The machine couldn't agree or disagree. "This was long ago, and the records have been corrupted. But no, it appears as if the skimmer you want has not been sold and not been taken away either. 'Vanished' is the word that I see."

"And how long ago?"

"Are you able to envision one million years?"

"Of course."

"That is a beginning," the voice said. "Now count another nine million years, and fifty million more after that."

7

First moments didn't exist, but the last instant remained vivid. Yesterday was never as real as that final day with Her.

The one-hundred-and-third coupling and a quick feast of electrified fats led to the woman's marching orders. They were on their way to a city called Between Here and Nowhere. Someone needed help or advice with difficult tasks that the two of them could manage, if inspired by suitable money. The job's specifics were always lost, but not the taste of the meal, which was ordinary, or the taste of the cold air between her palatial skimmer and his relatively simple vehicle. A considerable amount of helium was mixed with the oxygen, and there were too many stars to remember all of their names, and Kingfisher breathed because he liked the action, even though humans had already adapted to anaerobic metabolisms. He sucked at the cold thin pleasure of the still air and listened to his boots on the ice and to the ice grinding so that his bones carried that noise to the ears, and then stepping aboard his skimmer, he felt something. Not a premonition, because premonitions would have changed his behavior. No, he felt the very slight wobble of ice that was at least half a kilometer deep, and eons of reflection and doubt had proved to him that some little bolide must have struck near enough to make the ice cap ripple like a drumhead.

He could have measured the disruption but didn't. She was already underway, and the odds of trouble seemed too slight to calculate.

Her skimmer was so quick and powerful, and she was the same. It was always a chore to keep as close as he wanted to be. Every day was a chase. She claimed to enjoy winning every day's race, and there was considerable evidence that she being honest. Pride and a self-absorbed soul and status and wealth. Each was a quality that she had in abundance, and Kingfisher was chasing what he had to catch, thinking about nothing else. Which very likely explained everything else that had ever happened to him, and ever would happen too.

The next bolide was not little and not distant. The ice and the water beneath Kingfisher didn't just exist for the convenience of life. They served as buffers to everything that fell onto the ship. In that distant age, sometimes the sky brightened when the largest objects were inbound. Defensive arrays could split apart the invading comet or some mountain of cold iron, lessening the risk to the hyperfiber below. That was what happened that day. Kingfisher saw the flares above and considered doing the very unusual, reaching out to the starship's central communication system. Which was still operational, yes. But first he shouted to his lover, telling her to be careful. "Rough weather," he said, which wasn't adequate as anyone's final words.

Then she called back to him, saying, "Hurry," and maybe quite a lot more.

But the impact was close and not far behind him, and the flash turned the world to steam. Kingfisher's skimmer rose high and came down spinning and temporarily dead, and Kingfisher was dead inside it. Those two factors would have normally amounted to very little. But the dead skimmer let its hull get breached, and boiling water poured into the cabin and took both of them under. For eighty-eight years, they lay on the bottom of the ocean, inside the Ganymede ice, waiting for the repair team to find them and give just enough aid to leave them despondent on the still-liquid, still-warm surface of a shrinking ocean.

"There was a woman with me," he told the robots, the AIs. But neither group knew anything about any women. Then he spoke to the engineers in charge of the project. "She was ahead of me, and the impact was behind, and she should have survived."

"She should have." The ranking engineer was a towering alien, a harum-scarum, speaking through his breathing mouth.

"Where is she?"

A scaled hand reached for Kingfisher, twin thumbs turning his head one direction, then the next.

"Search for her please," he said.

Then the harum-scarum said, "We have searched without realizing it. Since the repairs started farther from the blast zone, and we've been working our way inwards ever since."

"So she escaped," said the human.

"Unless there's another explanation," his companion warned.

"As in?"

"Do you know what hyperfiber is?"

"Of course I know. Why ask such a thing?"

The engineer said, "We were hammered by a moon-sized object. Our ocean barely slowed its descent. You don't want to hear how much of the hull was damaged. Let's focus on a shard that wasn't much larger than your tiny hand, intact and accidentally sharp as only hyperfiber can be. That razor shard crossed hundreds, maybe thousands of kilometers at a fraction of light speed. And judging by the evidence, it's only purpose was to catch you below your monkey jaw, cutting through the skull and your bioceramic brain, and then happily flying on.

"You have healed remarkably on your own, sir. But some wounds won't ever repair themselves."

"What are you telling me?"

"What are you asking me?"

"I know what hyperfiber is," Kingfisher repeated. "I know what my name is, I know how to pilot my skimmer and speak to you in full, compelling sentences. And I understand that you think that I've been left an imbecile."

"Not an imbecile, no." The harum-scarum let him go. "But about this woman of yours. I wonder. Is she real in every way, or real only upon this torn-apart mind of yours?"

8

Ice and the cold were lost. The City That Needed No Other Name was vast enough to make its own weather under a shimmering sky full of flyers and song. Broad slow filthy rivers drained the distant interior, and keeping to the shadows, keeping alone for as long as possible, Kingfisher walked to a river pier and boarded the first swift liner heading upriver. Then sitting as far from the other passengers as possible, he woke the last of his working nexuses.

Linking to agreeable channels, he announced, "I have items to sell. Rare treasures from the far reaches of the world."

A multitude replied, and where he saw promise, he surrendered details and a plea for bids.

The long cabin was filled with aliens. He recognized a young Sun-of-Need, three Pilldogs, and one Janusian couple. But unfamiliar species dominated, and he had no urge to approach any of them. Yes, it was disappointing to hear about the millions of years between him and his lover. But this was undeniable progress. A slow, methodical search would give him results, maybe some rich clues, and best of all, centuries filled with promising work. Kingfisher wanted to roam the City, and for far longer than just a hundred years. That's why he needed to sell the trash acquired on the ice, and that's why he was disappointed when no substantive bids arrived. What if his valuables were true garbage? That was another question to be delayed. Another tough decision was delayed, and after paying passage to the river's source, he bathed himself in security and fed himself his finest sedative, passing across those next thirty hours in one spectacular blink.

He woke abruptly.

A woman was holding his hand.

She was human. Maybe. But then she let that warm human hand change its nature, and he didn't know what she was.

Kingfisher pulled back.

She laughed at him, at his fear and disgust. Then she was purely human again, smiling as she said, "Panwere."

"What's that?"

"My species' name."

Kingfisher didn't care about alien names. His security bath was inoperable. That's all that mattered now.

"I protected you," she said.

Or left him exposed. But at least his sack of treasures remained sealed and encrypted, dangling from his young left hand.

"Do you need a guide?" she asked.

"When I don't know where I'm going," he said. "But I always know, so I don't help."

"Fair enough."

Kingfisher shifted his rump, creating distance.

She laughed at that too.

The river liner was approaching its final destination, the long cabin empty of passengers, everyone below, ready to disembark.

"So where are you going?" she asked.

Kingfisher refused to answer.

She refused to drop the topic. "Because there's no City like the City, and someone as old and innocent as you are—"

"How do you know what I am?"

"You're the man who made a public call about artifacts and then left your position exposed. You're the man who sounds and acts and smells like someone who has wandered the wastelands until there's nothing but pack ice and solitude inside your skull. And in the City, that sorry kind of entity will be mistreated and abused until he hovers near death."

"Maybe that's my goal," he said.

The false face was watching him. She wasn't laughing now.

Horns roared, the liner grabbing the final pier, and Kingfisher picked up his body and his bag, walking fast until she caught up to him. Then he stopped, hoping she would pass him and move on.

But the panwere creature just stood beside him.

"Here," she said.

Six objects that belonged inside his bag rode inside her cupped hands.

"These are the only valuable items. Null-cores and nonfunctional quagmires from unknown aliens. They fell on your faraway ice, and you thought they looked neat or pretty, and that's why you foolishly brought them along, exposed. But I kept them safe and you safe when the thieves came sniffing."

"What thieves?"

"The ones you slept through."

He unsealed his bag. Its familiar weight came from slugs of iron and one dense bone stolen from an alien finger.

She asked, "Why do I want to help you?"

"I don't know why," he said.

"No," she said. "The correct response is, 'I don't care about reasons. But I am thrilled that you are here, looking out for me.'"

Kingfisher started to walk again, reaching the ramp leading down to the pier, and the alien was close beside him, deftly slipping those six stolen items back where they belonged.

They were the last two passengers to leave. "I know a responsible buyer," she said. "Offer those six baubles now, with proper documentation, then ignore the curses and settle for the buyer's third and last final offer. I'll show you how to stow them inside an approved locker, waiting for their new owner. And as soon as that's done, you'll have funds enough to fly both of us to ten thousand destinations, in luxury."

Kingfisher stopped under the brightest lamp.

She stood beside him, close but not close. An hour passed, and another hour. Not one word was spoken.

At last, he asked, "What sort of payment do you want?"

"Stories," she said, the smile returning again. "Tell me where you have been and what you have seen and what you know for fact and by legend."

"You want to hear about the ice?"

"Yes," she said.

Then she laughed once more, saying, "Plus my gracious help deserves one sum every five point five days. And with that rate, there are no negotiations."

He made a face.

The human hand touched him softly. "Did you really believe you can win anyone with just your words?"

Kingfisher stepped back, but he already missed the feel of those fingers against his lonely cheek.

Maybe that was why he agreed to her terms.

More likely, it was greed.

The relics were sold, the transaction happening exactly as promised. Then trying to shepherd his modest wealth, Kingfisher booked passage for both of them on a slow public cap-car. There was no conversation. No stories or questions and certainly no explanations about the alien's nature. Silence seemed like the most natural state between them. But he finally made himself say, "You must have a name."

"I most certainly do."

"What do I call you?"

"Whatever you wish to call me."

"And do you want to know my name?"

"If it helps," she said, laughing hard. "Particularly if it helps you tell these extraordinary, fascinating tales of adventure. Why not?"

9

The emerald skimmer had vanished. That's what the AI dockmaster had told Kingfisher, and there was no reason to assume otherwise. But Kingfisher needed to see where the machine was once stowed, and he was compelled to stand exactly where his love stood, staring out across the ancient, doomed ice. The City of Thieves. The City of Monsters. The City Ploughing Straight Ahead. Hyperfiber prows and picks were far below his feet, chiseling into the frozen whiteness, creating pockets where sonic drills and superheated rivers could enlarge the fractures. But the simple relentless mass of this huge metropolis did most of the work. Newborn crevices reached a thousand kilometers ahead. Kingfisher felt certain about the number, though he couldn't say why. Tearing ice had a predictable thunder, which he knew quite well, and he watched thick wedges rise sideways and lengthwise, standing ten kilometers tall before shattering along every weak line. Which resulted in a different, more musical roar. Then those little cubic-kilometer bits were shoved on top of one another, fighting to avoid the City of Annihilation. Slush and ice and sound were wrapped around complex mathematics, creating a temporary wall that kept the bow submerged. Kingfisher was standing on a seawall made from hyperfiber. The silvery wall rose two kilometers tall, and every sliver of shattered ice and every agitated drop of meltwater was pushed under the bow, sliding down to places where the City of Heavy Engineering could swallow everything inside a sequence of gigantic mouths.

"This was my job," he said.

His guide couldn't hear him over the thunder, and he didn't show his lips to her. That's why he made the confession.

"I was an engineer before I was mutilated," he whispered. "A great expert in hydraulics, with a specialty in a certain line of pumps."

The panwere was standing on his left, watching someone else approach.

An antinoise screen was deployed, and inside that abrupt, perfect quiet, a new voice whispered, "May I help?"

A human male stood on Kingfisher's right. He could be any age, but ancient was most likely. It was the way that he did nothing but stand, perfection mastered by the infinitely patient legs.

"This used to be docklands," Kingfisher said.

"And it will be again, whenever the City makes a significant change of course."

Every city coastline bristled with intakes and engines, helping to make these vast creations simpler to steer. Not gracefully easy, no. But at least you didn't have to pull on a wheel and force a five-hundred-kilometer rudder into some new direction.

"Was this dock your facility?"

"Yes, sir. And it still is."

"The berths are mothballed?"

"Under the hull over here. As soon as we reverse course, the ocean falls away, and I leave my retirement behind."

Kingfisher glanced at his alien guide. Did she have questions for this man, or perhaps insights for her new employer?

Apparently not.

"An emerald skimmer," said Kingfisher. He started to give codes and details, but the man interrupted.

"I know it well, sir."

Which was puzzling. "You know it yet you lost it."

"Who claims that I lost anything?" The ageless fellow couldn't straightened his back anymore. "'Reliable as the day is long.' Have you heard that expression, sir?"

"I think I have, yes."

"That is me, sir. 'Reliable as the day is long.'"

"But that cliché makes no sense to me," said Kingfisher. "Days aren't long. Years aren't long. Centuries are little more than nothing."

"But every good day is exceptionally long, sir. If you allow it the chance." The retired dockmaster spent a good moment studying the panwere guide, making assessments. Finding no reason for caution, he said, "The concept 'lost' is popular with AIs and other machine minds. Objects thinking about objects. That's what they are. And objects always crave to be labeled and properly stowed. But we humans, we understand . . . something can be out of sight, and maybe something vanishes in one manner or many others . . . but that is nothing like being truly lost."

Kingfisher was ready with one question, but another confession fled from him instead.

"I feel lost."

An honest assessment, and what could be said?

The dockmaster shrugged.

Again, one question was ready. But the lost man couldn't make himself ask it. Turning, he watched that wilderness of shattered ice and the distant towering peaks. Without noise, the majesty had been transformed. Free of thunder, every watered face of ice became lovely and weak.

"Where is this City heading?" asked Kingfisher.

"I am not our captain. I can only guess."

"So guess."

"To the end of the world, or nearly so."

The guide saw some reason to laugh, and she didn't pretend to sound human. It was a chittery giggle, and the two humans looked at each other.

"The emerald skimmer," Kingfisher said again.

"Yes, sir."

"Is it still stowed in its berth?"

"A berth paid for from now until the end of the universe. Yes, sir."

Kingfisher entered this moment expecting bliss. All of these ages, all the relentless endless thankless chasing, had come to this. But the opposite emotion was what arrived, ambushing him, the surprise nothing but cruel. Legs that had held him upright for millions of years failed him. No time had passed and he was sitting on the walkway, stricken and cold. Every human had his heart. In easy times, the organ helped the blood move, and that four-chambered muscle was a useful marker proving that its owner was a member of an ancient, wondrous species. But the organ served mostly as a gauge of emotions. Its beat and the pain inside the chest told quite a lot, and this particular roaring heart threatened to burst, promising to kill itself just to accent the man's utter misery.

Kingfisher's guide knelt first.

The touch of three fingers was welcome.

Then the dockmaster knelt, putting his face level with Kingfisher's face. "I believe you," he said. "I have never seen any creature more lost than you, sir."

The pounding heart did not slow.

But Kingfisher's voice sounded remarkably calm. "So she stowed her craft and left the City by other means," he said.

"No," the man said.

"But she eventually left you. Correct?"

"Hardly."

Then the guide spoke, her mouth changing shape to accommodate a string of chirps and pops.

With his human tongue, the dockmaster said one name.

Kingfisher watched the two of them nodding, exchanging some vast understanding coupled with surprise.

"So my love is still here," Kingfisher decided.

But the City of Nightmares was vast, and there must be millions if not tens of billions of humans scattered among the aliens, and that meant more years of searching before the end.

"Here, yes," said the man.

Then the panwere touched Kingfisher with hands and lips, his forehead receiving those small affections while the mouth once more became human. And quietly, tenderly, she told him, "She is our City's captain. She is the Master steering us on this course, as she has since the day after the day she arrived."

10

"Before this existence, I had the most splendid life."

Those words. She often said those precise words, and then after some delay, more words obediently followed behind. His lover had many,

many tales about terrible loss and tragic suffering, as well as passionate, inventive curses directed at long-ago foes. But Kingfisher never put his arms around those words. He might be standing beside her on the ice or sharing the air inside her palace of a skimmer. Sometimes he was inside her bed, laying quiet while she sat beside him, looming over him, screaming about the unfairness and idiocy of a universe that would allow her to be cheated out of everything that she cherished. But there wasn't one memory where Kingfisher gave a good shit about what the woman had suffered or what was stolen or the color of her grief or the darkness inside her dreams. He worshipped her present life, which was still magnificent. And yes, his brain was mutilated, forgetful and leaky and odd, but he was quite certain that he never felt anything but utterly jealous towards the so-called splendid life that cursed her existence, and his.

They coupled one hundred and three times. She said Kingfisher's name ninety-two thousand and nine occasions, by his count. That feminine voice was rich and booming, exactly suited to giving orders, and it was the sound and the energy of her voice that he focused on whenever she roared. The passions of a god were washing over little Kingfisher, but the words didn't give a shit if they were understood. Words were practiced noise, none of them possessing a soul, and indifference was Kingfisher's secret skill. This was why he could remain beside her for so long. Woeful tales about impossible places, duty orders and criticisms, plus the silences that sometimes stretched ahead for years. That was what he endured. Nearly a thousand times, he was invited into her bed, which meant that most occasions brought nothing but poor sleep and pretending to listen. He never touched what wasn't offered, and he was exceptionally good at remaining still, careful to nod and careful to say, "That is sad," or, "I wish it wasn't so." The lies of every devoted lover, and the man never felt wrong or foolish. Or vindicated. Or reliably happy either.

Then there was a very different aeon, and another bed.

Kingfisher's own skimmer was a sleek machine spun from diamond webs, holding twin reactors than never failed. The best repair AIs, the finest recyke systems. And an automated pilot incapable of mistakes. But no system was eternal. The skimmer announced that it couldn't continue. Too many portions of its elderly body needed fixing, and after a decade of dedicated searching, Kingfisher found a village capable of the work, and at a reasonable cost.

The village called itself Gracious, and for three years and thirty-eight days, he lived nowhere else. But because every roof sported sails, the community was always sliding along the ice with the prevailing winds, moving in a direction not too different from how he wanted to move. That's why Kingfisher felt that the chase was still on. Any progress meant that he slept well, and he ate every meal with strangers who turned into friends, and there even a few humans among the citizenry.

These new friends had no choice but to learn a lot about Kingfisher. Never a creature to hide emotions or his goals, he asked each about the giant human woman and the emerald skimmer. Had they seen both or heard stories about either? They hadn't and they hadn't, but maybe they knew about other villages or little cities where a devoted man could corner the amiable, better traveled citizens, pumping them for valuable information.

Every hour, without fail, some smiling voice would ask, "Is success even possible, so much time has passed?"

Almost every day, some elder would touch the traveler gently, then a wise voice would suggest, "Maybe, sir, you need a different quest. Maybe you need to forget more of your murky past. Maybe you deserve better for your life, sir. Maybe the one you chase is not the one you deserve."

That talk meant nothing. More practiced, soulless words. That's how Kingfisher felt then and always. Each of those possibilities was easy to spot and just as easy to set aside. No, he remained a creature of focus and endless resolve.

There was one unattached human woman, and he eagerly slept with her. There was no reason to count the times, much less chisel the details into his brain. This was biology. This was warmth and companionship that was finer than what machines and imagination could render for a man, but not markedly superior. This wasn't a tenth as fine as the very strange wife Kingfisher would take with his tenth long-term pause in the search. This happened between his third pause and his fourth, and during their last night together, his bed partner made it her mission to stop him from leaving.

Obvious old tactics failed in succession. But then again, she was just trying to numb him to her true plan.

She repeated several of his favorite stories, and then invoking logic, she said, "You don't love the mystery woman. You love the chase."

Not untrue, and why would admitting that stop him?

"I can imagine loving you," she promised.

"Can you?" he asked.

She said nothing. Then she said, "Yes." Then she silently watched her bedroom ceiling. A picture of stars taken in a much different age was on display, and the best she could offer then was, "I'll love you better than she loves you, you idiot."

The idiot had to laugh at that.

He thought that he was strong and smart, but no, he had fallen into her trap. The woman turned her face to look at him, and then her entire body spun about, and with a strength normally kept hidden, she took hold of Kingfisher's wrists and pulled the forearms together, her face dipping until she could suck on the tips of each of his fingers and then both thumbs. Then she sat up again, and with a sadness that would ache inside him for eons, she said, "You know. You do. That you have forgotten so much, what with time and that accident.

"But has that broken head ever asked you this question:

"'What compels a man to cross the infinite ice, seeking out the lady who left him for dead . . . the lady who has spent a hundred million years conspicuously and forever leaving him behind?'"

11

Two companions accompanied the hunter to meet his destiny. They shared one fine reason, which was curiosity. How often did this kind of situation arise? Not just in the City of Magnificent Coincidences, no. But onboard this marvelous pseudosphere starship, or anywhere inside the universe where it roamed? This was an event without precedence, and if either one of them was a social creature, he or she would have brought a crowd of friends and tag-alongs on this sudden journey to the City's bridge. But it was just the two of them, and it wasn't just curiosity that they shared, but also a measure of tenderness. Who couldn't feel sorrow for this broken, lost, and very odd human pursuing ends that made so little sense?

The Master was on the bridge, as she always was.

And she was guarded by security troops and munitions, and more dangerous by far, a cadre of machines and machine-like organics whose existence was wrapped around the Master's well-being.

Public offices led to quieter offices, and then a sequence of waiting rooms and cavernous lobbies where underling after underling would emerge long enough to ask the same questions and record the some variation of the same responses before retreating for realms that no ordinary creature would ever see.

The obvious took an embarrassingly long while to be seen. But Kingfisher finally realized that these workers were deeply curious about the mysterious visitor. The story that he needed to tell more than once had already been retold by others many thousands of times. Kingfisher was the unexpected dressed in novelty. He was the most unique event to come into these busy important but generally changeless lives, at least since these creatures were children and delightfully innocent. Even the name, Kingfisher, was a subject of considerable interest. One nobody with minimal clearances and zero authority knelt before him, and proud about his talents, he showed the hunter and his two partners an image pulled from the most ancient database. A blue monster called a kingfisher stood in brilliant sunshine, bright amoral eyes gazing across generations and millions of lightyears, decidedly unimpressed by whatever it happened to see.

The second to the last interviewer was a soldier, a harum-scarum trained and happy in his duties supplying protection to a woman who needed no protection. That's why he was charmed when the traveler asked to see his ornamental sword. And then this Kingfisher mentioned that he liked the blade and the feel of its weight, and could he hold it until the end of the work day? Its presence made him happy.

Here was an emotion every harum-scarum would understand. "I will return at the end of my shift," the alien promised. "Hold it tight and be strong, sir."

Another underling emerged from the main bridge, but this was not a small creature pretending importance. She was the last wall between him and her Master, and since every decision had been made, every permission already granted, her only duty was to stand at a distance, reminding each of the three entities that they were in the presence of a busy soul who was giving them too much time and they should be pleased for this honor, and they needed to be polite, and if her Master wished, the conversation might, but only might, continue into a quick dinner. But nothing more. "And you should expect quite a bit less," she said.

She was a panwere, like Kingfisher's guide.

Then her mouth changed, insect creaks and pops emerging and then fading again.

The two aliens might have been laughing.

The retired dockmaster understood enough to join in with soft chuckles.

And Kingfisher sat with the sword, making ready. Many times today, during conversations but particularly during the quiet times, he had realized the truth. This journey, his great chase, had never been about love, of course. No, he had traveled halfway across the universe and across billions of kilometers of ice in order to murder the woman who abused him and then left him and presumably forgot him many times over. But until now, that reason was lost. Lost because he was damaged, yes. But more importantly, lost because the blunt fact couldn't be confessed to anyone. Nobody would help an assassin, even if his cause was just. So Kingfisher had invented his devotion, and the lie took hold inside him. Words never had souls, but with the ages, the man making those practiced noises had no choice but to believe what he said, claiming to All that the hard beating of his heart was linked to a great enduring love.

Too many times today, Kingfisher had decided to kill the woman. Except the security was heavy, and his hands were empty. So no, his first plan was say the expected words and smile and maybe weep a little, then retreat, going off to make slow, delicious plans, using his fresh little wealth to buy weapons or build traps that would bring revenge.

But was murder best?

The sword was acquired through a fluke. This weapon was intended for show, all but harmless even to weakest immortal. But what Kingfisher decided next was to rush the awful woman, using steel to carve out her heart and then somehow carry that muscle away. As a trophy, as a hostage. Maybe as a warm salty dinner. That kind of insult would kill no one, but it would be satisfying. Wouldn't it be?

Surely, yes.

But no.

Then the panwere arrived and spoke, and then she returned to the bridge, promising the Master's appearance inside the next few moments. And with the calmest voice inside the calmest of skulls, Kingfisher said, "No, I'll cut out my own heart. That I can do easily enough. Slice it from the rib cage and fling it at her face. She will remember that. They will all remember that. And best of all, it's something that I won't ever forget."

Then the giant doorway opened.

Patient slow feet approached.

Kingfisher gripped the sword with both hands, practicing the surgery in his head, making himself an expert.

The Master came into the room alone.

She looked at the three visitors, and with a perfect memory woven from a multitude of nexuses and linked AIs, she said, "I know two of you."

But not the man in the middle, she implied.

Which was very reasonable, since Kingfisher had never seen this woman before in his life.

12

Midway through the tenth pause, when Kingfisher felt as happy as he could ever feel going nowhere, a world came to visit. The ark was small and ancient, and more than most of its kind, it was wrapped tight around its own existence. The last long ages had been spent in the ocean below the ice. An upwelling of oxygen and several equipment failures lifted into a fissure within an easy walk of Kingfisher's front door. He ignored its presence until the fissure closed and froze hard, and what else was possible? Kingfisher put on heated clothes and came out to sit beside this little mountain of diamond and vacuum floats and dense organic matter meant to replicate an entire biosphere. But as usually happens with arks, the world had one voice and a single attitude honed by living forever in the pressurized cold far below.

What must have been eyes watched him and watched the sky.

"To where are we traveling?" asked that shared voice.

"Nowhere from what I can tell," he said. "But the ice is trying hard to shift, and you'll get torn loose. In another few years, with luck."

The voice said, "No."

Sexless and quiet and a little sad, perhaps, it said, "You misunderstand."

Then every eye stared at the perfect blackness above, and those little blemishes of blue light clustered closer to the sky's heart. And the same question was asked. "To where are we traveling?"

Kingfisher decided to say nothing.

Then the ark said, "We were told where. A human once explained quite a lot to us, and would you like to hear?"

"No," he said.

But they told it anyway. They claimed that there was a time when the human species was still quite young and a cold machine of endless worth was found abandoned and taken by human hands. But other creatures stole the treasure and then flew it far away, and this galactic ship, this vast pseudosphere astonishment, was built to give chase. Passing worlds were invited to send arks to the ship, which was a superior means of building diversity while acquiring every sort of the strength. This ark claimed that somewhere in that blueness was the only treasure worth possessing in the universe, and one day it would be found and recovered, and it was such a comfort for a soul, knowing that there was purpose to life and an end was coming.

Somewhere inside that telling, Kingfisher stood and walked away.

The human-voiced wife spoke as he entered his home. She said his name twice and asked what the ark wanted, and he picked up one tool and then asked for an item that wasn't in the first locker or the second. But here it was, hiding in the third locker, and he thanked her for her help, and she said in her very pleasant way, "I didn't help at all and be careful."

The ark watched him return.

That shared voice asked, "Is that a bomb?"

A uranium bomb with a heated sheath, yes. Which they recognized and there was no reason to say anything else.

Kingfisher engaged the device and set it down, and as soon as it had vanished into the ice cap, he put the plasma drill against the smallest of the ark's vacuum floats. The hyperfiber was stubborn but not invincible. He quit working only when the ark mentioned violence, and only to tell it, "This will put you back at neutral buoyancy. I think. And don't dare threaten me again, or I'll blow the bomb early and your voyage comes to an end."

There was a long, frightened pause.

Or maybe the ark was calm or at least resigned to its fate. Who knew with such a strange amalgamation of genetics?

When Kingfisher was finished, stowing the drill back into its box, the ark repeated what it said earlier. "A human told us where we are going."

"Was this human female?"

"No."

"Was she a giant female?" he asked.

The voice said, "No, and no. The human was masculine and not large."

The nuclear charge was deep enough now. A signal arrived, and the expectations of an order.

Kingfisher gave no instructions.

Then the ark said, "This was so long ago. Memory is a fluid and fills any bottle it's given and we are a bottle in every sense. But the male human that we remember had your face and your voice."

"You're right," he told the ark.

"Yes?"

"Memory is water, and water flows where it wants."

Then he retreated just far enough and set off his very expensive bomb, for no reason but to make the ark leave him alone, and the ice was still shaking when he returned to the house and the woman and the darkness inside every silent room.

13

A day like none other mercifully found its end, and another fifty-eight days followed, quieter by comparison but never easy or small or quick to finish. A giant human lady had been charmed by this stranger, and because of that or because it was so very easy, she gave Kingfisher access to old records that might not be more than a little corrupted. There were three emerald skimmers registered in the central files, he learned. The tag-numbers that he assumed were important were exactly that. But each of the three vehicles wore the same numbers, and there was no way to know where the other two were just now. But because it might help to learn about their whereabouts, the Master ordered her emerald skimmer taken out of storage and transported back across the City Pushing to the Edge of the World.

"You need a better vehicle for your chase," she told Kingfisher through a messenger. "Find the lady you want so much or my colleague with the third skimmer. Then send me word, if you can. This voyage has pushed on far longer than anyone imagined, and every big thing is a mess, obviously, and I could use any help before trying to bring order to this big stupid nearly useless ship of ours."

The emerald skimmer was exactly the same as the one he remembered, except when he stared for too long at any wall or doorway, and then every tiny detail proved that this wasn't his enemy's at all.

Sometimes he cried while walking those long hallways.

But mostly, he trembled with excitement for the coming voyage.

His guide remained with him to the end, paid her fee and a bonus too. Kingfisher had considerable money, most of it in the form of gifts from wealthy aliens that had too much of everything but novelty.

Kingfisher and the AI dockmaster stood watching the quiet water behind the City That Never Rested, and then the human turned to the panwere. She had been his companion for fifty-nine days, which was no time at all. They had touched on five occasions since the first day, none of those gestures important. Yet he remembered each time and smiled for good reasons, and after a little while he said to her, "I have met your kind before. I'm assuming."

"There are a few of us, yes."

"Can you really take any form you want?"

"What I want is too much, so no." She laughed with that insect voice, then returned to tongue and lips. "But I enjoy quite a range of possibilities, yes. Within the limits of mass and energy and imagination and decency, yes. Everything is possible."

"I have had three ideas," Kingfisher said.

She waited.

"The first idea was that you follow me inside my old ship."

She showed him nothing with her face, but the voice said, "I won't."

"My second idea is to invite you to ride with me across the ice," he offered. "This wonder of a skimmer would be a comfortable home for us and anyone else we find along the way."

She began to say, "No."

But Kingfisher already put his finger on her mouth, feeling teeth and heat and spit too.

"No, the third idea is what I will do," he said. "I will go alone into my voyage, because that's the way it should be."

Down came his hand.

She said nothing.

"You are free," he said. "Go find another traveler to show around this City of Shifting Faces."

She said, "All right."

Again, he said, "I will go alone."

Then Kingfisher turned to the AI. "Sell my old skimmer. Then apply that money and whatever else you think is fair. Boundless storage for the emerald skimmer. That's what I am purchasing. I want the machine ready for me at a moment's notice, but that may not happen for a long while."

"Yes, sir. Very good."

Then alone, Kingfisher began to walk along the dirty slow dark river that kept pouring from the City's interior, and he was alone for exactly ninety-nine heartbeats. Then a hand took his hand, and looking nowhere but straight ahead, he said, "But whatever you do, never let yourself resemble Her."

ABOUT THE AUTHOR

Robert Reed has had eleven novels published, starting with *The Leeshore* in 1987 and most recently with *The Well of Stars* in 2004. Since winning the first annual *L. Ron Hubbard Writers of the Future* contest in 1986 (under the pen name Robert Touzalin) and being a finalist for the John W. Campbell Award for best new writer in 1987, he has had over 200 shorter works published in a variety of magazines and anthologies. Eleven of those stories were published in his critically-acclaimed first collection, *The Dragons of Springplace*, in 1999. Twelve more stories appear in his second collection, *The Cuckoo's Boys* [2005]. In addition to his success in the U.S., Reed has also been published in the U.K., Russia, Japan, Spain and in France, where a second (French-language) collection of nine of his shorter works, *Chrysalide,* was released in 2002. Bob has had stories appear in at least one of the annual "Year's Best" anthologies in every year since 1992. Bob has received nominations for both the Nebula Award (nominated and voted upon by genre authors) and the Hugo Award (nominated and voted upon by fans), as well as numerous other literary awards (see Awards). He won his first Hugo Award for the 2006 novella "*A Billion Eves*". His most recent book is the *The Memory of Sky* (Prime Books, 2014).

The Privilege of the Happy Ending
KIJ JOHNSON

This is a story that ends as all stories do, eventually, in deaths.

When Ada's parents died in the winter of her sixth year, she was sent to the neighboring parish to live with her aunt, Margery. Margery was a widow with three daughters, all older than Ada; and their names were Cruelty, Spite, and Malice. They lived in a narrow cottage with a single room, and rain came in where the thatch had grown thin beside the falling-down chimney. Margery had a garden and a pig and some piglets, and three sheep, though one was old. There was also a coop full of hens with a single rooster. There was no room for an orphan in Margery's narrow cottage, nor in her narrow gray life, so Ada slept in the coop surrounded by the chickens: their feathers and fluff, their earthy smell, their soft nonsense gabbling—and of everyone in that household, Ada's food was scantiest but her bed was softest.

Ada loved all the hens, but her favorite was Blanche: white as a pearl and sturdy as a peasant's ankle, with five bright white nails on each ivory foot, a beak the pink of rosebuds in May, and a flat little comb and wattle the crimson of full-blown roses in July. She was pretty as an enameled jewel made for a duke, yet her golden-black eyes were clever as clever. Blanche's egg-laying days were past, but it was Ada's task to collect the eggs and tell her aunt who was laying and who was not; and so Blanche was not eaten.

There was a day after the hay had been brought in but just before the fringed golden wheat was ready for the sickle. After Margery and the sisters broke their fast, the porridge pot had been nearly empty (and the rest needed for dinner); so once Ada had fed the hens and collected the eggs, she went into the old forest to find something from which she might make her own meal. But she knew it was dangerous to go alone, and so she took Blanche.

The road became a path as it crossed into the shadows of the old forest. Ada was gleaning sweet musty blackberries and bitter-bright burdock greens (too late in the season, but there they were, and thus worth trying) until Blanche saw the feathery little leaves of kippernuts tucked close to an oak tree's roots. Ada squatted to dig the tiny tubers from the ground, and carefully brushed them free of dirt. She had two for each one Blanche took, which they agreed was only fair, for she was bigger and had done the work.

Ada had eaten six-and-twenty kippernuts (and Blanche thirteen) when they heard someone running along the path-that-was-a-road. The news that comes on fast feet is seldom good but is always important, so Ada leapt up, and Blanche scurried from her bug scratching to press close, peeking past her legs. But it was just a boy that burst into sight, heaving and panting and out of breath: older than she, thin and dressed poorly (for *he* was an orphan as well), and running on bare feet beaten hard as boot-soles.

When he saw Ada, he paused, gasping until he could speak at last. "Where. Is your mother? I have. News that is. Worth. A penny or more."

"I have no mother, but I have an aunt. She lives that way." Ada pointed along the path.

"Is there a. Village? I don't want to. Waste my time."

"There's a church and a miller *and* a blacksmith," said Ada, looking up at him. "What news is worth a penny?"

"Do you *have* a. Penny?" said the boy.

She shook her head. "I have a chicken, and I have this pin. My mother gave it to me before she died." She pulled it from her collar to show it to him: fine as a hair and straight as a thread pulled tight, with a tiny silver knob at one end.

"A chicken's too heavy," he said but plucked the pin from her fingers, though she had offered neither. "It's wastoures! They came through Newton and Blackhill and killed everything, and then they split into two big groups and one turned north, and the other's coming here. I stay ahead of them and earn pennies by warning people."

Wastoures. Perhaps you have not heard of them, you people born a thousand years after Ada and Blanche and this runner—whose name is Hardourt, though his part in this story is nearly over: his name will not matter to you, though it matters to him. In your time they are gone, but in the twelfth century, every child knew of them, and adults as well. Wastoures: scarce larger than chickens but unfeathered and wingless, snake-necked and sharp-beaked and bright-clawed, with little arms ending in daggery talons. For long years there would be no wastoures (except in memory and dread), and then a population bloom, like duckweed choking an August pond, or locusts after a dry spring, or cicadas rising from the ground each seventeenth year. For reasons unknowable, they emerged in their scores of thousands from some unknown cave or forgotten Roman mine, and seethed like floodwater or plague across the land. Eventually they died off, plunging heedless from cliffs or drowning in waters too deep to cross; or else autumn made them torpid, then dead—but not before they had eaten every breathing creature they encountered. They were in everyone's nightmares, and small children feared them more even than wolves or orphanhood. These were dark times, wastoure summers.

Wastoures. At the sound of the word, Blanche fluttered into Ada's arms. The girl shivered and said, "Take us home! Please, I'm too little to run fast enough by myself."

He eyed her. "You're too big to carry. How far is it?"

"Very far," she said sadly. She had walked all morning and now it was early afternoon. If she ran home—if she *could* run so far—she would not get there before the midwife's cow began complaining to be milked. And Margery would not notice her absence until dusk, when there would be no one to chivvy the chickens to their coop. The wastoures would catch her before that.

"Then I can't take you," he said. "You're too slow. They'd catch us both and eat even our bones."

Ada knew hard truths. She was raised in them. "Take Blanche, at least."

Blanche clucked and tightened her feet, pinching at Ada's arms.

The boy snorted. "What, that? It's just an old hen."

Ada fired up indignantly. "She's the cleverest chicken that ever was! And she talks."

"Lying is a sin," said the boy; "You're a crazy little girl"—though he was not so much older than she.

She freed one hand from Blanche and pointed down the road. "At least go to my aunt and my cousins and tell them? And the priest and the blacksmith. I'm sure there are *many* pennies there."

"Good luck." The boy took off running, and did not slow nor look back. And now he is gone from this story.

Ada stood in the path-that-was-a-road, tightly holding Blanche. When the patter of running footsteps had faded, there were no sounds but the humming insects and the air soughing in the forest. She looked back the way the boy had come, but there was nothing to see yet, only trees and plants: high above them all the towering clouds of August, uncaring about the tiny affairs of people and hens and wastoures.

"What should I do?" asked Ada aloud.

And in her light, sweet, gabbling voice, Blanche said: "We must climb the highest tree and wait 'til they're past. He told the truth. They're coming."

Did you think that Ada had lied to the boy to save Blanche? She is a very honest girl. Because no chicken has spoken within your hearing, do you assume none ever has?

Ada put down Blanche and they looked about. The old forest was dense with staunch oak and shivery beech, saplings and shrubs, coiling ferns and little low groundling plants. Everything was either too big to reach or too small to save them. Ada hopped for the nearest branch of a low-slung oak, but it was much too high.

Blanche said with decision, "Not here, but there will be Somewhere."

Was that a sound? Yes. It was the ripple of running water, where a brook ran along the bottom of a clearing clotted with grasses, and encircled by young trees. Across the clearing was a pile of stones that had once been a house: French or Saxon or Roman, or any of the races that had swept across England's face. Gone now, all gone: absorbed into Englishness, into legend and folktale.

Was that a sound? Yes. It was a rising wind in the trees, from the east. Ada carried Blanche through the head-high grass to the pile of stones. It was ringed by nettles but she paid no heed, only pushed through and heaved Blanche to the top of a fallen wall. (Marjory had clipped each hen's right wingtip, and Blanche could not fly but only flutter.) Ada crawled up after and hoisted Blanche onto an overhanging elm tree branch, but she could not reach it herself.

Was that a sound? Yes. It was a great red buck crashing through the underbrush. Ada saw him flash across the clearing, wall-eyed in panic, heavy-footed and careless of sound. Blanche said, "Stack the stones," and so Ada did, heaving onto the wall the biggest she could move until she could climb to the top of her teetering mound. She jumped for the branch and scuffled her feet up the trunk to sit at last beside Blanche on the rough gray bark.

"Higher," said Blanche, and Ada climbed, up and up, and the hen jump-fluttered along. Up and up, until the branches creaked ominously and bobbed like osiers from even their small weight.

Was that a sound? A scream, or sudden wind, or a cart wheel complaining? Ada looked but there was little she could see, only elm leaves and a bit of the clearing, and one glimpse directly down, of the pile of stones and the ground, a great way below.

Blanche said, "Let me see what *I* may see." She hop-fluttered to the tippiest branches of the tree.

Ada peered after her. "What *do* you see?"

Blanche said: "I see sky and clouds. I see the sun setting, and the steeple of our own church: that's the west. I see a flock of birds rising where something has frightened them: that's the south. I see trees moving in the wind and I see smoke from chimneys. I see trees moving, and it is *not* the wind. *That* is the east. I see smoke from a thatched roof burning. I see a meadow covered with darkness, and the darkness is coming toward us."

She hopped back to Ada. "I see wastoures. Use your shawl to tie us to this branch so that we don't fall in the night. They are coming."

Was that a sound? Yes. A low wail, a storm-sound, a surf-sound of chattering nattering shrieks, louder than crows in their murders and rooks in their parliaments, louder than a myriad of hawks fighting for blood. A thousand talons pounded the ground. Blanche ruffled her feathers and buried her face in Ada's arms, but still the sound.

The wastoures came. The trees shook and the tall grasses shivered, first from animals fleeing, every deer and mouse and marten and vole running for its life, but then from the wastoures themselves. They trampled the grasses as they poured like a flood across the clearing, eddied wherever they found some living thing to eat, crashed against the trees and scoured the bark with their claws and talons, until swarming they swept past. But always more.

The night was bright-mooned, alas. Ada saw a fallow doe pulled down in her flight (for she would not run faster than her fawn) and skeletonized quicker than a hen lays an egg, and the fawn even faster than she. The wastoures swirled around a pile of stones in the clearing until they unearthed a fox den and ate the kits. There was a great anguished roaring in the forest, which Blanche whispered surely was a bear pulled from her hiding place and killed. The wastoures could smell Ada and Blanche, and some spent the night leaping at the elm tree's trunk. But wastoures cannot fly, nor could they jump high enough to reach that first low branch. After a while Ada saw that they could not get to her.

Hour after hour; the moon set, and still they churned below, a seething darkness in the dim starlight. Ada feared she and Blanche would fall, for she was not very good at knots yet, but nothing bad happened. She was only rocked gently like an infant in its cradle, far above the tossing sea of wastoures, and at last she slept, for a child cannot always be awake even in a time of terror.

But Blanche did not sleep, watching from her bright golden-black eyes.

By first light there were fewer wastoures. The crushed grass was red with dawn and more than dawn. The lingering wastoures bickered for the chance to pull the blades through their beaks, for the blood.

Ada whispered to Blanche, "I have to pee."

"So?" Blanche had no great opinion of the things people worried about.

Ada wrinkled her brow. "They'll smell it."

Blanche tipped her head as though listening through the feather-edged pinholes of her ears, though what she listened to was not the air. "By now, most are far to the west. These are the little lame ones that cannot keep up. They'll leave soon enough."

"They don't seem any littler than the others," said Ada, dubious, but she peed over the side of the branch anyway. One came sniffing over and looked up, eyeing them from its sideways-tipped head before it ambled off to the west. The others followed.

Ada was very hungry (for burdock and blackberries and a handful of kippernuts had been yesterday's dinner, and today's breakfast, too). But still she waited until Blanche said at last, "We can get down now."

"Are we safe?" said Ada.

"We are never safe," said Blanche.

It was worse descending. Blanche flutter-jumped from branch to branch, but Ada had to lower herself carefully, and the bark that had seemed so sturdy under hands rushing up now broke away under the same hands creeping down. The lowest branch was higher than she remembered, and it was a long time before she could bring herself to drop onto the tumbledown wall.

At the sound, one final wastoure emerged from a pile of fallen stones. Not all the blood drawn in the long night had that of forest creatures; this wastoure had been slashed accidentally by a fellow and itself became prey. It limped toward them, hungry and curious, but Blanche spread her white wings and snapped her short rose-pink beak. To her surprise it turned away and limped westward into the forest.

And now *it* is gone from this story as well. Imagine its ending as you would. If you are kind, see it dead quickly in the jaws of a hungry young wolf a short league from this place. If you are as cold as the world, then see pain, infection, hunger, and death a mercy at last.

Ada picked up Blanche and recrossed the clearing to the path-that-was-a-road. The wastoures had crushed the ferns and trampled the shrubs, gouged the beech and staunch oak with their claws, scattered blood and shards of bone everywhere—but the road home was easy to see, for the deep-trenched ruts were a thousand years old, more permanent than any horde.

It was afternoon when they came at last to the forest's edge and saw their little church across the trampled fields, and the handful of houses and huts, but the chimneys were unsmoking and the doors agape or gone. There was no sound: no churn or quern or clattering loom, no hammer on iron or chisel on wood, no oxen or horses, milk-cows or sheep or chuckling chickens. Ada had always been a little afraid of the village's big dogs, and even more afraid of the geese, but neither came buffeting down the lane to bowl her flat.

Marjory's cottage was at the far end of the village. Three was-toures had clustered around something gray and red in the lane between *here* and *there*. They did not look up.

"Will they eat us?" whispered Ada.

Blanche said, "I think they are no longer hungry."

Perhaps she was right, for they sidled into the woods, leaving their dinner half-eaten: Father Alfred's donkey. Blanche fluttered from Ada's arms and ran across to peek through the gaping door of the nearest cottage, where Ada's only friend Giles lived, with his siblings Armand and Geoffroy and Natalie and Marie, their mother and father and aunt, five goats and a dog, two cows, and the chickens and ducks.

"Is anyone there?" asked Ada.

Blanche said only, "Do not look inside the huts. Do not look closely at anything."

Everywhere was the same. There were corpses or parts of them, and sometimes Ada could tell who it had been. Other people were just not there and there was no telling where they had gone, or how. The donkey was partially eaten, but his short gray face was for some reason untouched, and his eyes were closed as though he were sleeping. Ada had always longed to stroke his nose but she had been scared to put her hand so close to those long yellow teeth. Now she stroked it at last, and it was as soft as she had guessed, like kitten ears.

You ask, Where is her grief? Why does Ada not scream and wail, as you might, or I? Why does she not fall to the ground in despair, run weeping in circles? She has seen horrors before this, horrors at six, orphaned and alone. She has been here before. She has learned that adults always fail—if only by dying—so what's new?

At least she has Blanche. Not every lost child does.

The door to Marjory's cottage was closed but the thatch had been torn through and the oiled oxskin that glazed the window was in shreds. When Ada reached for the door, Blanche pushed her white head between hand and iron latch. "Best not," she said.

The coop door was agape, and the sunlight streaming in filled the air with golden flecks. The chickens were gone, dead or fled or hiding deep in the hearts of trees they had managed somehow to ascend. There were only torn nests, broken eggshells, and splashes of blood clustered with busy flies; but the air still smelled comfortingly of Blanche's kin, feathers and fluff, millet and shit.

And what of Blanche's grief? Do you think she feels none? I have known a chicken who pined to death, waiting by the gate for a dead coopmate until she starved. But sometimes grief is a luxury. But Blanche is practical, and there is Ada to look after.

Ada's little bed of hay and rags had been ripped apart. She plumped it back together and cuddled down, with an eye on the open doorway. Blanche tucked herself carefully onto her favorite roost, just above, and said: "We must plan."

They could not stay. Wastoures did not come every year, but when they did, it was in waves. Tomorrow, the day after, next week—they would come again, and keep coming until winter came and they died or found secret caverns. Also, there would be scavengers: foxes, rats, and others on two legs, scrounging through whatever was left behind. Ada would not be able to hide here.

There was no point to following the wastoures' path, for everywhere they had been would be the same: ruin, loss, the clustering scavengers. And the lands they had *not* yet touched would be overrun with fleeing people and animals, lost or afraid to go home. No one would care for a small barefooted girl and a clip-winged white hen.

"What *can* we do?" Ada asked. She was drowsy with eating. They had gone out again and found food everywhere, in lavish and unguarded profusion. The wastoures ate only flesh, so there were tarts and turnips, cabbages and tender new carrots. Ada had filled her skirt with apples and bread (nibbled, for some mice had survived) and carried them back to the coop.

Blanche said, "Wastoures cannot swim. If we cross a lake or a river without a bridge, we'll be safer. Maybe. A town with a moat would be best."

"What's a moat?" Ada knew what a town was; it was more people than she had ever seen in her whole life, all in a place.

"A river that runs all the way around a town. A ring of water," said Blanche.

Ada nodded, as though she understood. "What do we do?"

"Find a new home. Find a family and make ourselves part of that."

"I suppose," said Ada, dubiously. Her experience with families was not so happy as Blanche's.

"First you must do a thing for me," said Blanche.

Ada nodded; she was so very tired.

Blanche dropped to the floor beside Ada and stretched out her right wing. "Pluck the clipped feathers."

Ada sat up. "But you won't be able to fly!"

"I cannot fly now. If you pluck them, they will grow back whole."

"How long will that take?" Ada asked.

But Blanche did not know, for it had never happened to her. It was only a sort of legend in every henyard. It was an uncomfortable business, for Ada was afraid to hurt Blanche and it required a strong pull, and Blanche could not help twitching away, but at last it was done and there were four feathers piled beside Ada's bed. By that time it was dark.

And, because Ada was after all a very small girl (and Blanche a chicken), in spite of the dead, the smell of blood and the loneliness, they slept. They could not have in any case kept their eyes open, not even if the wastoures had run ravening in and devoured them down to the bones.

In the morning, Ada filled a basket with white bread, a hard cheese wrapped in a cloth, and butter in a tub she had found sunk into a pail of water at the midwife's house—all finer than anything she had eaten since coming to Margery's cottage. She did not think to bring a knife nor money until Blanche reminded her (Blanche was old for a hen and accordingly wise), and then she took a dirk and eleven silver pennies from the blacksmith's house, and put on a blue gown that had belonged to his middle daughter—for her own was ruined and there was no sign of his family, no sign at all. They walked south into the new morning.

A small girl and a hen are not built to travel fast nor far, especially when they must often hide. Their path traversed the wasteland the wastoures had left behind: ruined fields and orchards, collapsed huts and trampled copses. Pillars of ravens and rooks circled above the wastoures' leavings—but even amid all the ruin were places that had not been damaged, as though the wastoures had been a wildfire, razing one field and leaving the next untouched.

They passed a village the wastoures had missed, but there were men with bows and short swords everywhere about it. "Leave it," said Blanche. "That is no home. We'll find somewhere better."

They saw other people like themselves (but adults), lost and stumbling or moving with fierce purpose. Some carried food. Others carried things that made no sense: a mirror, a silver candlestick, a roll of vellum, a fine cape too warm for August. Once there was a woman with her head uncovered and her hair a tangled mat down her back, cradling a bundle and weeping; she saw Ada and folded to her knees, reaching out, and the bundle dropped forgotten from her hands: not a babe in arms but a crumpled wad of rags. Later a man chased them, snatching for Blanche until she attacked, flapping into his face; and he stumbled back with a scream, hands laced over his eyes and blood seeping past his fingers.

And now *they* are gone from this story, as well, the blinded thief and the grieving woman and these other hard-faced or frightened roamers. I have not told you their stories. They do not matter; they die alone, unremembered, pointless except to make a point. All authors leave a swath of destruction. We maim and move on. The privilege of the happy ending is accorded to few.

That night, Ada and Blanche slept in an empty sheepfold under the bright-mooned sky. In the morning they went on, though the soles of Ada's feet burned with the friction of calluses on dirt. In time they came to a brook. Ada lay down on the bank, paddling her feet in the cold water as Blanche scratched for worms.

"What do we do now?" Ada asked.

Chickens do not much note the expressions of people, but even to Blanche the girl looked pale and tired. She dropped beside her and rubbed her small feathery face against Ada's.

"There will be a place for us. I know it."

The wind shifted, and as though she had summoned the sound, they heard the distant sound of church bells: a single low bell rung nine times, then a pause, then nine more.

Nine, and nine again. Blanche said, "Nine tolls for a man, and seven for a woman—" the distant bell was tolling seven; seven; seven—"and three for a child of more than four years."

Ada was six. "What if you are smaller?"

Blanche's voice was a soft clucking. "For an infant, a single bell to remind men of the soul reaped early, and to comfort the mother."

Three, three, three: a long pause, and then a single toll.

Blanche said, "Someone still lives, to climb the church tower and pull the rope. There is order there. *That* is where we must go."

"Will they want us?" Ada asked, for Marjory had not.

Blanche smoothed a feather with her beak, heaved herself back onto her sturdy claws. "If they do not, we must find a way to make them want us."

They followed a sunken lane, smooth with use and pounded smoother by the recent four-toed prints of wastoures. They hid from a youth limping the other way, and from two hard-faced men dragging a high-piled handcart. They hid from a double file of silent monks bearing a dead man on a litter, and from a half-grown wild boar so lost in the pain of its torn flank that it stumbled unseeing down the middle of the lane. In the afternoon, Ada shared the last of her bread with Blanche, leaving the pot with the remains of the butter at the base of a beech tree, for even ants grow hungry.

They were still trudging along the lane when the bell tolled again, so sudden, close, and loud that all they had to do was turn left and climb a hill. And there was the Unlucky Village.

Perhaps the wastoure's numbers had been greater here, or their hunger. From the breast of the hill the village seemed no more than huddled ruins: houses and cottages destroyed, stone walls and chimneys toppled, roofs collapsed. The outbuildings were torn apart entirely, and only piles of stone, thatch, wood, and withy marked their locations. The fences had been trampled into the ground, the gardens razed. A wasteland of stained, crushed grass was all that was left of the common green. Only the little parish church looked intact, though the lead roof had buckled in one corner. The bell had fallen silent again.

Blanche scuttered a few steps down the path to the village, but Ada did not follow. Seeing this, Blanche said, "Come," in the tone that had once brought her chicks running (grown now, grown to hens and cocks: grown, gone, and dead).

Ada chewed her lip. "No."

What is the hen's equivalent of a sigh? A puff of breath and an impatient shake of wattle and comb? Blanche gave it. "It will be night soon, and there will be wolves and bandits and perhaps wastoures, too."

Ada's head shook, *no no no*, though she did not seem to realize it. "There's nobody here."

Yet there was white smoke rising from a chimney, and the sound of iron on wood, and the drifting scent of an oak wood fire and barley porridge on the boil. Blanche sighed again, that complicated act, then harried Ada down the path, the girl stumbling and her lip trembling. But what choice did they have?

They passed the first fallen fence, and at last they saw someone, a woman leaving one of the ruined cottages to hurry across the green.

Ada did a very brave thing then. For all her fear, she called out, "Wait!"

The woman did not stop, only averted her face as she ran past, vanishing round the corner of a paling half-erected to surround the church. Blanche fluttered into Ada's arms, and they tumbled after her and saw other people now: a woman stacking wood salvaged from a ruined house, a man digging a grave. Another, holding a paling upright in its hole, looked up grim-faced, but he also said nothing, and turned back at a sharp word from the man trying to set the post in the ground—as though that would stop the wastoures when they came again; as though anything would.

Ada stood uncertainly in the middle of the claw-flattened lane. "What should we do?" she whispered, though she knew that Blanche would not speak in front of these hard-faced people. The hen in her arms only shook her head.

"Who are you?" asked a voice, unexpected and very close. Blanche fluttered to the ground with a squawk, but Ada looked up into the face of a man they hadn't noticed. He had been rehanging a nearby cottage's door; he still held a mallet and the new-forged pin for the hinge.

Ada looked at Blanche for advice, but the hen said of course nothing. "Are you ghosts?" she asked at last.

The man put down his mallet and stepped back from the door. He was very tall, and wore dusty black shoes. "We look it, I guess," he said. "Are you?"

Ada shook her head. "No, I am a girl, and this is Blanche. She's a hen, not a ghost either."

"You're alone?" The man walked across.

"No!" said Ada, indignantly. "I have Blanche. But we don't know what to do."

The man looked down from all his great height for a moment, then knelt and reached out a hand to her. "You might stay here with me and the boy. I'm Robert. I have room for you if you want it."

After disaster, when we are adults, we survive if we can. We are hungry, we are cold, we are sick or injured. We save what and who we can. There is fear, loss, and crippling grief, but we do not have time or energy yet to fully reckon our dead. We must think about tonight and tomorrow: portioning out the phone's charge and our only bottle of water, tallying the last seven doses of our heart medication, now six, now five. Periods start whether we have tampons or not. Diapers need to be changed even when there are none.

But someone will come. We will hear helicopters, trucks, see red crosses and crescents. We will be safe.

When we are children alone in the heart of horrors, we do not know this.

There had been no warning for the Unlucky Village, no boy earning pennies until he felt the wastoures' talons scything the air at his heels. Robert had been a farrier (but the horses were gone) and a husband (his wife, as well: walking back from the Egendon market where she had gone to sell her weaving) and a father (daughters dead with their mother, and his son in the churchyard's fifth new grave). Robert was an old man, though he had not been so a week ago.

He gave Ada the loft his children had shared. "But no chickens inside," he said, so Blanche slept in the henhouse, which was empty except for her own quick heartbeat, for the wastoures had found them all. Each night Ada crept out to cuddle with Blanche, until Robert brought her back in.

There was another child that he had found: a boy a little older than Ada. The day after the wastoures had passed, Robert had gone searching for his wife and daughters, though he found no signs of them but a ribbon that might once have been blue. On his way back, he heard a hopeless, unaware moaning from within the hollow trunk of a fallen oak tree and opened the trunk with his axe. There was a boy, wedged as deep as he had been able to get. His right foot was shredded where the wastoures had worked for a while at pulling him out. Robert brought the boy home and laid him in his own bed. The boy's name was Ulf, though Robert will never learn this.

This, then, was Ada's family in the Unlucky Village: grieving Robert substituted for bitter Marjory, raving Ulf for the cruel sisters, and Blanche. There was plenty of food (though no meat) and blankets enough for everyone who was left. Robert was gone all of each day, trying to set the fields to rights without oxen, guarding against looters, working on the paling—for always the Unlucky Village worked in fear of the next wave.

It was Ada's job to watch the porridge pot and the fire, and also to watch the boy. When Robert was not by, Blanche crept in and sat with her. Her plucked feathers were growing back, little sharp quills so delicate she could feel air moving like fingers on them.

Watching Ulf was not an easy thing. He was feverish and kept reaching down to paw at his leg above the ruined foot, where it was mottled the color of marsh water. He gabbled *Mother* and *Father, Jesu* and *Mary*; the names of his sisters and brother, his dog, and his family's cows.

On the second day, he started up in his fever and grasped Ada's arm with a hot hand like a claw. "You don't belong here," he hissed. "He's *my* father now."

Blanche flared her wings and snaked her white neck forward, but before she could peck him, he had released Ada and fell back delirious again, crying and repeating, "The Lucky Village, the Lucky Village."

Blanche settled on Ada's knee, one wary golden-black eye on the boy. Ada whispered, "What's the Lucky Village?"

Blanche contemplated, in the way she had. "It's a true thing. There is a village where the wastoures don't come."

"Is it a town with a moat?" asked Ada.

"No," said Blanche. "It is just luckier than others."

"Where is it?"

"Somewhere near." Blanche kept no maps in her head, though she could find places once she knew they existed.

"Your chicken talks?" said the boy abruptly. He had a habit of sudden lucidity.

Ada said, "No."

"I know it did! I'm sick but I'm not deaf." He pushed himself upright in the bed.

"You dreamed it," said Ada fiercely, "and if you tell Robert, I will stick you with a pin"—for she had forgotten that the running boy had taken the pin her mother had given to her. But when Robert returned at dusk (and Blanche in the yard, meek as a nun, as though she had never seen the inside of a house), the boy had fallen back into terrors and seemed to remember nothing of their talk. A line had begun creeping up the boy's leg like a streak of oak-gall ink, ankle to calf.

"He's going to die," Blanche said softly once when they were together, and Ada nodded. She remembered the smell from when her parents had died.

But Robert did not know that smell, or chose to ignore it. The boy would be fine. He needed time. He needed herbs. He needed charms hung over his bed and painted upon his leg. He needed to be kept cool, to be kept warm, to be pouliced with nettle infusions, to sleep, to be prayed over. The line crept up and up. When Ada could not sleep for the sound of the boy's sobs, she crept into the henhouse and cuddled Blanche close, nose deep in her sweet, earthy fluff.

On their third day in the Unlucky Village, there was news: a boy not running but trotting loose-kneed with exhaustion, who told them that a wave of wastoures had passed in the night, to the north. "Is Woodend safe?" asked a woman whose daughter had moved there to wed; but the boy shook his head.

"I started in Berton, and I ran through Tirborne and Nutley and Chatton, and I hid in a tree when they went past, and now I'm going back. I came past Woodend last night. There was nothing left." He thought. "Nothing to recognize."

But the woman was screaming already and she beat him with her fists until two of the men pulled her still screaming away; and instead of staying for the night as he had hoped to, the boy left—though with a wallet full of fried porridge-cakes and new apples slipped to him (but secretly) by one of the other village women. For it was not *her* bad news he carried, and it might have been.

Now, this boy also is gone from this tale. He will return safely to Berton with thirty-two pennies, apprentice himself to the blacksmith (who has lost all his sons), and in time become blacksmith himself. He will have three daughters and two sons, and mourn his first wife when she dies in childbirth, but not so much that he will not wed again. He will not have nightmares. He will not dream. Horror does not strike all equally.

That night Robert said, "The boy needs meat."

He and Ada sat at the little crooked table beside the fire, eating porridge stiff from a day's cooking, with hazelnuts and some lettuces that had survived the garden's ruin, and drinking small beer. Ulf had rejected everything. He tossed in the corner bed, moaning in his sleep.

"There is none," Ada said sadly. Her mouth watered as she thought of stewed beef, duck meat pressed until it was tender, trout fried and sizzling; the sweet flesh of such chickens as were not Blanche.

Robert gestured outside. "We have the hen." Blanche was pecking for insects just beyond the cottage door; she looked up, her white feathers aglow in the sunlight, plump, bright-eyed, and hale.

Ada shook her head.

He rubbed his eyes. "We have to be reasonable. It isn't laying and it'll have no chicks. And the boy needs to eat. A good broth, some stewed meat—"

"No."

"He's *sick*, girl. We need to get him better."

"He's not going to get better," said Ada: too young to know what should not be said. "He's going to die anyway."

Robert slammed his fist on the table and stood, and the room loomed with his shadows, cast from firelight and the late sun shining in through the door. "The boy will be fine!" he said.

Ada began to cry, and Blanche scuttered through the door and flutter-hopped ground to bench to table, and launched herself at Robert's face. Robert threw up his hands to protect his eyes and grabbed Blanche by the throat. She hung, fluttering and squawking.

72

"You can't eat her," Ada cried. "She is a talking chicken."

"Lies are the Old Gentleman's work," Robert said sternly.

But Ulf had been awakened by the fight, and said, in the quick feverish voice that came in his moments of clarity, "It does! I heard it yesterday. And *she* said she would stick me with a pin if I said anything." He jabbed a thin finger at Ada.

"Hens do not speak," Robert said, and held up Blanche to look at her, no longer struggling but hanging loosely in his hands. Blanche gave a sudden writhe and dropped to the table, and said:

"If I did, would you not eat me?"

This was the end of Ada's family in the Unlucky Village.

Robert stopped his ears against Blanche's words and Ada's tears, and dragging the girl to the coop, threw her inside, the hen scuttering protectively after her; slammed the door shut and left them there. A talking chicken *must* be some trick of the Devil. It might even in some fashion attract wastoures, for hen and horror were likewise two-legged and claw-footed, snake-necked and bright eyed. In any case, Robert had no room in his life for things he did not understand yet could not ignore. The hen would be killed and made soup of, that was understood, though first the priest must expel any demons, lest they enter the boy. That would be a task for the morning. The girl would get over it. What choice did she have?

But in the night, as Ada clutched Blanche tight in her arms, the hen said to her, "We must go."

"Where?" asked Ada. "Everywhere will be like this."

A chink in the back wall admitted a blade of steel-colored moonlight. "The people of this village see nothing but badness. The Lucky Village will be different."

"Will it?" said Ada dubiously. "Shouldn't we go to the Town With A Moat?"

But even a talking hen that sees truths may ignore them, and decide instead that the easy path is the only one. Blanche said, "The Lucky Village will be fine."

The coop had been built to keep chickens in and foxes and weasels out; still, fear and fingers found a way to pry loose a board in the back. It was noisy but no one of the Unlucky Village (not even Robert) opened their tight-sealed doors to learn what new ill thing the sounds augured.

Ada squeezed out, and Blanche after her, and for the rest of the night, they hid in a ravaged cottage nearby. At first light, they started to walk. There was no food and no blankets, only the eight remaining silver pennies and a shawl which had once belonged to Robert's oldest girl, which he had given to Ada, soft as a chick and blue as an August sky.

The raving boy, Ulf, will die in two days and be buried on the third. Robert will die later, and it will not matter when or why or how, even to Robert.

Blanche and Ada walked for a day and another, and in the night between, they slept in the house of a woman who said not a single word, only wept steadily as November rain, even while she put out fresh-baked oakcakes and honey for them both and arranged a blanket into a little nest beside the fire. Though there was room enough and the walls were firm, neither girl nor hen spoke of staying. In the morning, the unspeaking woman gave them the last of the oatcakes and a skin to carry water in.

Things happened, horrors and little beauties.

When it seemed prudent, Ada asked after the Lucky Village, but no one had heard of such a place until an ancient man mumbled past his five remaining teeth, "That'm Byfield." He pointed with a finger so bent it seemed to turn back on itself. "'Along o' there. An' east o' the Hangin' Cross an' west at the River Bye an' on for five, six miles. But they don' like strange folk"—and he pointed to a scar on his arm, many decades old.

On for five, six miles. They ate worms and honey cakes, purslane and dandelions, and berries from inside a bush where the birds had not gotten to them. They ate beetles and a loaf of barley bread that Ada purchased from a blank-faced man with one of her pennies. They grew hungrier. They hid. They hid. They hid.

At last they came to a narrow lane with a signpost Ada could not read, but—"This way," said Blanche. They turned and came down through a copse of oak trees between fields amazingly untrampled.

And there it was. The Lucky Village was cradled in a curve of a clear, swift-moving stream, and the green before the gray stone church was clustered with fat sheep—for in these troubled times, it seemed safest to keep them close. There were chickens (though none who spoke) and geese and even a farrowing sow. There was a parson and a miller, a blacksmith and a harness-maker, a baker and a woman who gave herbs and treated injuries, a man who rented out his strong back and a woman born foolish who could not speak—and what was her use in the village none would say (though we guess and do not guess wrong).

The Lucky Village had never been attacked by wastoures. They did not understand what accidents of landscape and circumstance protected them, so they interpreted their safety in their own way. They were lucky because they were good—but they also had to be careful: virtuous, discreet, cautious, slow to change, swift to assess sin and exact punishment. They were wary of strangers at all times, but during a wastoure summer, the Lucky Village turned everyone away, with weapons if need be.

Ada and Blanche were intercepted by a man scything a field and brought to the steps of the church to stand before the parson and the blacksmith. The rest of the Lucky Village gathered around them. They asked questions: What did a very small girl in a sky-blue shawl, carrying seven pennies and a chicken as white as a pearl, have to offer that they could not simply take from her (had they not been good men)? Was *she* good? Did she know her prayers? Did she honor the Church? Did she work hard?

Ada, confused and tired and hungry, wept.

The Lucky Village said, Well, we don't need more of *that*.

Ada scrubbed her eyes against her shoulder (for her arms were filled with Blanche) and said, "My chicken is magic. She does tricks." Blanche gave a sudden start.

The Lucky Village said, What sort of tricks?

Blanche was looking as wary as a chicken can look, head tipped sideways to see Ada fully from one golden-black eye. Ada only lowered Blanche to the stone stairs.

"Blanche, count to nine." Nine was a lucky number.

Blanche tapped the stone delicately with one ivory-nailed foot. Nine times.

It's a sham, said the Lucky Village. You always say nine, or you gave her some secret signal.

"What is three plus four, dear Blanche?" said Ada.

Blanche spread her wings and resettled them. Arithmetic was hard until she imagined beetles scuttering across the ground and snapping them up, first three, then four. Seven.

Exclamations; a spattering of hands clapping.

"And she can dance, and she can talk, and she can tell the weather. But she will only do it if you let us stay."

The woman who gave herbs to the Village knelt. "Poor little things!" she said. Her voice was kind. "You may stay with my husband and me. We have never had children."

"And no one will eat Blanche?"

No one, promised the Lucky Village.

It all looked very much as Ada's little home had looked. Her new mother and father were kind, if stern, though they gave her much to do and

75

were very serious about her prayers. In her home with her own parents (before they died), Ada had not yet learned the church-word prayers, just little English rhyming versions; after their death, Margery had not cared much about Ada's eternal soul, but now her new father demanded she learn the *Pater Noster* and *Ave Maria*, and he beat her when she was slow—though not hard: a swat merely, to keep her alert. Blanche, who was always close by, ruffled up at this but did not peck or claw.

Even on the warmest afternoons, Ada wore the blue shawl and carried with her the seven pennies, her little knife, and some bread—for after leaving the Unlucky Village, she had learned to keep close everything that was hers, plus whatever food she could. Her new mother gave her an ancient mended leather pouch for this purpose, to reassure her until she settled in.

There was a bed for her inside the cottage, but Ada slept with Blanche in the coop. "It's not right," said her new father, but her new mother only said, "Peace, husband; she has seen things. Give her time." And so it was permitted (for now), and in the meantime Ada learned the church-word prayers and worked hard.

There were other chickens. None of the chickens of Margery's flock had ever spoken save Blanche, but who knew the natural rules of talking among chickens? Not Ada. When she asked Blanche, the hen disdained them all as silly creatures saying nothing worth hearing. But this was the price for staying in the Lucky Village, Blanche knew: sleep safe, surrounded by fools who are not even kin.

In the long blue August dusks, the Lucky Village brought out a rough table from behind the alehouse and placed it on the green, and Blanche hop-fluttered onto it and answered questions. At first she only added numbers for them, tapping the worn wood with one white toe.

Then the Lucky Village asked, You said it talks? That it tells the morrow's weather?

Ada and Blanche looked at each other. Robert had cast them out for speaking at all, let alone foretelling anything: why should the Lucky Village be any different? For Ada had not lied: The weather *was* one of the truths that Blanche knew, though she had never bothered to speak of it before the wastoures came. It could not be changed and she'd had her coop to retreat to, so why bother? But it had been useful as they wandered, since the wastoures.

"Yes," said Blanche finally. Her voice was a sweet gabble that cut through the rattling twilight insects and the never-quite-gone murmur of the Lucky Village's talk. "Tomorrow will start foggy down by the stream, but it will clear, and after that it will be hot and bright. The trout will stay cool in the hollow below the willow tree. The bees will cluster on the goosefoot and the meadow saffron. Beetles will hide, but the little grass-snakes will lie in the sunny lane and be easy to catch."

Exclamations, uneasy laughter, surprise. Some thought Ada spoke for Blanche through a clever trick, though she was very young to have such skill. A few groused that anyone could predict all that at this season. One or two wondered whether this was the Devil's work. But on the whole, the Lucky Village was pleased. Knowing the weather was indeed useful, and perhaps this hen was yet another proof that they were not lucky but blessed.

Days passed. On the Feast of St. Alcmund, wastoures seethed across the countryside a few miles to the south. Jesu preserved the Lucky Village, yet again.

A few days after that came a running boy, warning of another wave from the west, half a day away and headed straight toward them. He made no pennies from the Village for, safe in God's arms, it knew it owed him none; and in any case he was a coarse, ill-favored child that stirred no compassion. Cursing them for heartless, he turned to go, but Ada ran after and gave him one of her pennies. Now she was down to six.

His name is Piers, this running boy. He has a birthmark shaped like a hare on his face, and an expression in his despairing eyes that no child should bear. His ankle hurts, from when he stepped on a rock and it shifted underfoot, but he still can run. How likely is it that he survives? How real do you want your fiction?

In the indigo twilight after vespers that night, the Lucky Village crowded close to Blanche. The nights were growing cold, so there was a bonfire that cast a shuddering light across them all. The Village would be fine, of course it would—though there were some who thought they might have shown more compassion to the running boy, given him bread at least.

Naturally we trust our benevolent Lord, said the Lucky Village. But. Is there anything we should be doing, anything more? Are we failing at anything?

"I am a hen. If you want sermons, go to Parson John," Blanche said, a little tartly, for her new-growing flight-feathers were itching. Parson John paused from sweeping the first fallen leaves from the steps of his church, just in earshot though not a part of the ring of listeners. He was one who believed Blanche was a temptation instead of a reward, but he trod warily. His flock's willingness to be led was inconstant in wastoure summers. They might cast *him* out.

Well, say *something*, said the Lucky Village.

With what was very near a sigh, and knowing they found comfort in such things, Blanche spoke the church-words Ada had been learning. *"Ave Maria, gratia plena, dominus tecum. Benedicta tua in —"*

"Profanation!" Parson John cast down his broom with a clatter that startled Blanche into Ada's arms; who stood beside the table. The Lucky Village exclaimed, murmured, and looked uneasily between man and hen.

"Did she get them wrong?" asked Ada: she was not as good with the church-words as Blanche.

"Abomination!" he bellowed, and the Village's murmurs grew louder, became mutterings. Ada's new mother stepped forward, but her new father placed his hand on her arm: safer to wait and see how this would arrange itself. The ring of watchers parted to admit the parson as he stomped to the table, stabbed a finger toward Blanche. She eyed his pointing finger rather as though she might bite it, feathers ruffled in the hot wind of his shouting. "A beast must not speak the words of angels!"

"She's not a beast!" said Ada, looking up, indignant. "She's a *chicken*."

The parson towered over her. "A soulless beast!"

Outcry; exclamation.

Parson John looked around the ring, and shouted, "Our Lord gave us dominion over such! And we throng to this beast, like the Israelites in the desert before the false idol of the Calf, and we listen to heresy. *He* will not forgive."

Ada's new mother stepped backward, into the circle of her husband's arm, and turned her face away.

This is how Ada and Blanche were cast from the Lucky Village that very night, into the path of the ravening wastoures.

What of the Lucky Village, cradled in a fluke of geography and conditionally cruel? You blame them for sending children to die alone. But they have their own. They must be prudent; they must be reasonable. They must make a choice, and so they do what is right for their own children, and not these strangers—though of course there *are* some that are merely cruel, or selfish, or too absorbed in their own fears to spare thought for others.

Their God does not seem to mind, but we little gods that are writers: we mind. Imagine the Lucky Village destroyed at last, if it comforts you. Or, if you are kind, imagine it learns its lesson and is rewarded with long lives and rich harvests. Imagine there is a lesson here. Still, why is fiction held to a higher standard than reality?

• • •

Dusk was fading into darkness. Ada fled headlong, for the men who had driven them away were still outlined by the bonfire with their cudgels and staves, and they scared her. Blanche scurried alongside, calling in her distress. They ran over the curve of the hill and then farther, until they were in a lane between trees, where not even starlight could reach them (for the crescent moon was not yet risen) and it was utterly black.

They ran until Ada stumbled, fell headlong into the unseen lane and sprawled there, grizzling and crying. Blanche huddled close.

"Hush," said Blanche, with the soft chuckling of a hen soothing her chicks; but her ears were open.

Ada wailed; she had hit her chin and was seeing stars, green flaring bursts behind her eyes, though it was so dark.

"Hush," said Blanche, but it was no longer a chuckle: it was a sharp snapping cluck.

Ada wept. She was six.

"*Hush,*" said Blanche, and this time it was a terrified whisper.

Ada's breath caught in her throat.

They heard it over their own hurrying heartbeats: still distant, the storm-sound of chattering nattering shrieks, the thunder of clawed feet.

"Not under the trees. Not like this. We must get into the open," said Blanche.

They stumbled through utter-filled utter darkness; and still the sounds, behind them and to their right. There were other noises now: splintering wood, branches torn, an animal's scream so tormented that it could not be identified as man or beast or bird. They tumbled on until they saw a lightening ahead, and suddenly they were out of the trees and fleeing beneath a star-scattered sky. The lane ran between fields too dark to see as more than textures, but smelling of barley to one side, scythed hay to the other. No houses, no lights, no shelter, no convenient tree; and still the sounds. Closer, louder.

There was a ragged wall on one side of the lane, a bit taller than Ada's head. "Here," hissed Blanche, and terror pushed them up the rough stones.

They crouched on the wall's top course, which was scarcely wider than Blanche's body. Everything was dark still. The gabbling sounds came from across the lane and beyond the barley field; as much as they could for the darkness, they watched the trees there. But now sounds came down the lane as well: a thundering of hooves and alarm-calls. A herd of fallow deer raced heedless in their hundreds, so close that Ada could have reached out and touched their heaving flanks as they passed. The wind of their flight smelled rank and peppery.

They could not see what pursued at first, but they heard them: the gabbling and screeching of wastoures. It was not the main wave, only a few score that had smelled the deer and broken from the larger group to stampede the herd. They hurtled past, and above them Ada and Blanche crouched, frozen, soundless, and as flattened as they could be on so narrow a perch.

The wastoures' heads were lower than the fence's top edge and perhaps they would not have bothered with Ada and Blanche, or even noticed them. But an adolescent bringing up the rear hesitated as it passed. It rocked back on its haunches, listening. Its head was a long dim wedge anchored with flicking eyes so pale they seemed to glow in the starlight. Ada was still as wax, yet it swiveled suddenly toward them. It scrabbled at the wall but couldn't get purchase, then opened its long muzzle to bare a fringe of sharp teeth and a hot rotting smell, and gave a call that was a cross between a kestrel's screech and the *tuk-tuk-tuk* of a hen calling her kin to food.

"Jump down on the other side of the fence," said Blanche. "Then *run*." But Ada did not move: calcified in fear, trapped tight as a chick in its shell.

After a moment, a larger wastoure joined the first. The smaller one sidled away, lowering its weight on its narrow hips and twisting its head to the side: a silent language unlike that of chickens, and yet Blanche understood it well enough. The higher-ranked wastoure clawed at the wall, long neck stretching up. Closer; but it could not reach, either. It lifted its head and called that screeching *tuk-tuk-tuk*.

Others loped back: perhaps twenty of those chasing the deer. Looking down, Blanche saw a swarm of backs and reaching necks and snapping long jaws. Ada still did not move, though her eyes were open and gazing at the milling wastoures.

They scraped and jumped at the fence. One, longer-necked, used its chin as a balance point to scratch its way up the wall, forelegs scrabbling along the stones. Blanche flared her wings and stabbed with her beak at its nearer eye, and it fell screaming down among the others, leaving a sticky smear of vitreous humor on the stone and the taste of slugs on her tongue. The swarm attacked the fallen wastoure, but the leader still watched Blanche, as though thinking something through. It made a sound, an abrupt clatter rising from its throat.

Blanche understood it well enough: no longer a sound that summoned others to food, but something like a hen's challenge-call to a strange pullet brought into her flock. She had not been lead hen of Marjory's kitchen yard without reason. She growled a chicken's growl, an angry rattle she had not had to make since her laying days. "*Back away,*" it was, and, "*Who are you to use that tone with* me?"

The wastoures went silent and retreated a little, leaving the shredded remains of the fallen one humped against the foot of the wall. Every wedge of a face angled toward her, smeared with blood that looked black under the moonless sky; every pale eye gleamed flatly, like a silver penny rediscovered in a dark corner. The leader snapped its head from side to side and chittered a clattering throat-sound: a clear challenge.

Blanche growled again, louder, and this time it was, "*Go.*" She opened her wings and stood tall: a rooster's stance. The leader reared in its turn, slashed the air with its gaping jaw, and chittered.

Was she afraid, fierce Blanche, facing down these monsters? The wastoures were taller, toothed, smelling of fresh blood, with claws sharper than a fighting cock's spurs; forelegs that reached and grasped in a way that wings could not. More: there was something of cunning in the leader's eyes. But Blanche was clever, too—and she was so angry that her fear was a mere background hum in her heart.

"*Go,*" growled Blanche, and she snapped forward with her beak, though the leader was too far away to peck. Nattering, the swarm recoiled. The leader lowered its weight a little on its narrow hips, still looking up. The dialect of its posture was unfamiliar yet understandable: confusion, wariness, skepticism.

Blanche looked down, small and sturdy and strong as a queen with a naked sword in her hand; and, hunched low, the wastoures peered back at her. She said, in words and hen-sounds and manner, "*Turn. Turn and run. Run until you drop in your tracks, run until you die. And do not return. Go.*"

The leader stepped backward, swiveled, and ran arrow-straight across the barley field. The others collected into a ragged mob behind it and vanished under the trees. In a moment even the sounds of their feet were gone. The only noise was the rustling of leaves: a night wind rising.

Ada still did not move, and when the hen pressed against her hand, it was cold as death. "It's all right, dear one," Blanche crooned. "They're gone."

The wastoures run, twenty-three of them, driven by a strange compulsion. They run and do not deviate, past farmhouses and villages; and when they come to the ford in the Wendle, where the water breaks knee-high on a riding-mare, they run into the water, lose their footing, and are swept away. Dead, as she demanded of them.

As for Ada, Blanche will not tell her that the wastoures have died. She is a child. She should not have to imagine how they fought the Wendle as it pulled them down, how their lungs filled with weed-foaming water, how their fear was as great as the world.

"What was *that*, hey?"said a voice behind Ada and Blanche.

His name was Pall, he told them: an orphan who with certain fellow spirits had cobbled together platforms in the trees where they could sleep safely. They were seven in number, and they scavenged for food and other things. "Why, we're rich!" he boasted to Ada, who had roused at his voice, begun crying, and now followed him, still grizzling, across the cut hayfield with a somewhat limp Blanche in her arms. "I have a silver candlestick, and three shillings and a lady's fine gown and a gold piece with a lion's head from some foreign land and a bridle for a horse and—"

The list was a long one, long enough to take them to the beginning of the forest. He stopped at the foot of a tree as he ended, "—an' I'll go to the King and he'll make me a lord, I'll be *that* rich.—Here."

He pointed to a rope leading up into the boughs.

"I can't." She started to grizzle again. Ada was a brave girl but she had just seen terrible things. Also, she was tired and hungry—and in any case, she could not climb like this: six and small for her age.

"Rules are, you have to climb to be one o' us Dead Squirrels," said he. "But still, that hen o' yours . . ." He gave a low whistle and a loop of rope dropped from the heights. "Put your arms through an' hold tight. I'll carry that hen."

"No," said Ada and held Blanche tighter, squeezing from her a squawk.

"I can take care of myself," said Blanche. Presumably, the boy had heard her speak already, so there was no point to concealment.

And so it was that they were lifted into the treetops, Blanche clinging to Ada's shoulder (and trying not to dig in too hard); Ada spinning and bumping until she learned to walk her feet against the trunk as they ascended. Pall shinnied up the other rope so quickly that he was already at the top to hoist her onto a rough platform scarcely bigger than her own little bed had been, back when there had been such things as parents and homes. A single candle in a horn-paned lantern cast grimy light onto the faces and hands of the boys as they sat in the crooks of branches or leaned back into the boughs. The oldest might have been twelve; the youngest was scarcely older than Ada.

"Why'd you bring 'em up?" said the Oldest. "We could have talked to 'em below;" and the Youngest wrinkled his face, adding, "They're not Squirrels!"

"There're still wastoures about," said Pall. "Seemed safest. They got *skills*, men. From right up here with your own eyes, you saw it. She sent 'em all away somehow, that hen."

"How'd you do that?" said a Squirrel, as another asked, "Where?" and the Youngest said, "Make them *all* go away!"

"I didn't send them away," said Blanche, who was literal-minded. "I only sent the chief of them. The others followed her. I think that's their way—like chickens, only not so clever." She preened a little.

Surprise at her soft gabbling voice. "You talk?" said one; while, "But what did you *do?*" said the Oldest; and the Youngest shaking his branch in excitement until leaves cascaded down into the darkness, crowing, "I saw! You stood up tall and flapped and shouted and they got scared and ran away."

"That hen," said Pall to the others. "She's got *skills,* see."

The Oldest Dead Squirrel looked down at them: Ada, curled tight in the exact center of the platform and still crying a bit; and Blanche standing beside her, small, round, and sturdy, her head tipped so that she could look back at him with one appraising eye.

"Can you send them away?" said the Oldest.

Said Blanche, "Yes."

"Well, then," he said. "You can stay.—But not if that'n's gonna cry all the time."

And after they tied Ada loosely onto the platform (so that she would not fall off in her sleep), each Dead Squirrel tucked himself into whatever nest he had fashioned in the branches close by, cradled in such wealth as he was able to rescue from the ruins of the world. The Oldest blew out the candle, for candles were scarce (wastoures ate tallow and wax), and in the darkness, the Dead Squirrels spoke. They had names from before or that they had given themselves: Pall and Red Paul, Stibby and Renard-the-Fox, Weyland and Edmund Blue-Toes and Baby Jack. Ada was half asleep and Blanche did not care about such things, and yet the names stuck in their minds and were not forgotten.

And they had stories: a monkey from the Holy Land that Stibby had seen at the last-but-one Michaelmas Fair (but maybe that was a lie); baby pigs that came when you called, and swallows that slept snug as housecats at the bottoms of millponds for the winter ("I saw it myself, so it's true as true," said Red Paul); digging out a badgers' cete in the spring (when sisters and parents still lived), and finding a scrap of tile old as old, painted with a single half-closed eye like a wink. As Squirrels nodded off, stories became whispers, became wishes. Family, family; home, home. No one said *safety.* They knew there was no such thing.

As for the Youngest, he told no tales at all, nor wished, but only cried silently now that he could not be seen.

Soon all were asleep save Blanche, tired as she was and late as it was.

It seemed that she could keep the wastoures away from Ada. Knowing this was like November sunlight in her breast. And Pall *was* right: she might be able to preserve these boys, as well. A roost in the trees might be home to hens, but people were not suited to it. Come soon, come late, they would need to come back to the ground where their flat sturdy feet served them so well, and when they did, she could keep the wastoures away from them, also.

Ada, safe. The Squirrels, safe.

And the rest. The boys who brought news, running for pennies until their feet or their hearts failed them. All the children: alone, or crowded with family into brief havens, or defended by parents who died before their eyes. And even the ones who would live long lives without seeing a wastoure, but were hunted across the decades in nightmares. All save the silent children already underground and feeding worms in the churchyards. For them it was too late.

The only way to protect them *all* was to stop the wastoures altogether. Was that possible?

There had been a leader among the wastoures she had sent away. Blanche's understanding of hierarchies was subtle in ways no human can fathom, but call it *alpha*. If the swarm that had trapped them at the wall was led by an alpha, then all swarms had alphas. Bring two swarms together, and there would still be just one alpha, for the lesser would fall back. So: gather all swarms together, and there would be a chief of all chiefs, an alphamost alpha. Send that one away and the others would follow.

Where would it be, such a leader of wastoures? And once she knew to ask, this was a thing she knew without learning, like the weather. She *felt* her, as iron filings feel a magnet: an aged uttermost queen whose cunning was as sharp and strong in Blanche's mind as the smell of yew in a churchyard. The way to the queen was as clear as *home* to a salmon in June: some leagues, south by southwest. She ruled in a cool damp cave of limestone that breathed the salt smell of a sea dead and gone long before hens or wastoures or any air-dwelling thing. Her court surrounded her, all the other egg-laying females, also grown old; and beyond them, the last lingering juveniles still too egg-tender to collect and ravage forth.

All of this sensing thrummed with the uttermost queen's demand to her flock: *grow/go forth/find caves and flourish/there is no returning.*

It was hard to comprehend but not impossible, in the way a traveler in a foreign land can pluck meaning from signs by their shape and placement. It thrummed like a pulse, like surf on a shingle beach.

Could she stop this uttermost queen? Blanche knew truths but not all truths; still, what choice did she have?

The night sky brightened as the crescent moon rose. It found a way through the leaves and shone onto Ada, who jerked upright, looking about wildly.

"Hush," said Blanche in her gentlest soft chuckling-to-chicks voice. "We are in the trees."

Ada nodded. "Are we safe?" she whispered.

"We are never safe," said Blanche. "But from the wastoures, perhaps. I know what to do."

Ada would not stay with the Squirrels, despite all her fear. She had been afraid since the day her mother died (and the baby with her), which had been five months after her father had died in the fields, cut almost in half by a plough. The people you loved failed you in a thousand ways, not least by dying out of your sight while you were doing what they told you to do, collecting walnuts in a basket or pulling weeds in the garden. After such lessons, who would not keep her eyes fixed on her last loved one? So Ada would not stay behind—and she would not again freeze in fear.

The Dead Squirrels did not want to let them go, but Blanche had a certain voice they all remembered, though their mothers were dead; and in the end, they lowered Blanche and Ada from the tree, with gifts: a stale honeycake they had been saving and a waterskin that was just barely manageable if Ada filled it only halfway.

The Squirrels: three will die, one by a fall, one of the flux, one killed by a man driven mad by this world. Which live? Which die? You have your favorites. Pall, because he is named and has shown kindness. Baby Jack because of his tender sobriquet, and we are sentimental about the young, though the world is not. The Oldest, though you do not even know which Squirrel that is, whether Weyland or Renard-the-Fox or even Edmund Blue-Toes. And if you knew that Stibby used to beat his little sisters and steal their food, and that Edmund once threw stones at a kitten until it died, would that change things?

The remaining four will live for a while, and then die, like everyone else.

Are you counting the deaths in this story, keeping a roster, keeping score? Is it higher or lower than *The Wizard of Oz*? There are more than I have told you.

• • •

Things happened, and other things.

Blanche and Ada backtracked along the path the wastoures had carved, past St Giles' and Coombe Pastor and what was left of Rufford. Everything was very lush from where the blood had soaked into the ground, and flies clustered like clouds at the thickest-growing places. Blanche scratched for her own food, but Ada needed more: bread at least (there was no meat or milk), and someone to help her when she got a sliver in her heel that she could not reach. She gave more of her pennies away, and soon there were only two.

At midafternoon on the sixth day, as the sky darkened with rain to the northwest, they came over the shoulder of a raw-rocked hill and saw a ruin in a clearing of the forest below them: the pale crumbling walls of what had once been a Roman villa, destroyed not by wastoures, but by weather and centuries of people stealing its stones for their own chimneys and fences—though it had been long ages since any had come to this place.

Blanche shivered. The uttermost queen was stronger now that they were so close, and her demands scratched at Blanche's mind the way growing feathers prickled in their sockets: *grow and go forth/eat/do not return/do not stop until you find new grounds/if you can.* Walking into the compulsion was like wading against flowing water, but Blanche marched on, and Ada close beside her.

They picked their way down the slope toward the villa. There were no plants beyond a few dusty shrubs, for anything smaller had been trampled flat by the waves of departing wastoures. There was no sound of living creatures, not so much as a fly; but when a rumble of thunder made them look up, they saw two birds circling against the heavy clouds. Blanche cast one golden-black eye on their braiding flights and knew them for carrion crows. Ada only wondered whether they had babies and how they kept them hidden.

A lone wastoure came suddenly around a collapsed wall, gawked, and gave a stuttering cry that was fierce cousin to the *tuk-tuk-tuk* of a hen summoning her chicks. A second popped from a hole in a leaf-covered floor. A third. More poured around corners and up from holes, and loped toward Blanche and Ada, calling. *Tuk-tuk-tuk.*

"I wish I had not brought you," said Blanche, but Ada laid her hand on Blanche's broad back and said, "Where else would I go?"

The first wastoure paused some paces away, wary and weaving, twisting its neck to peer from each eye in turn. *Tuk-tuk-tuk.* The others streamed past it, until—

"*Stop*," Blanche said, with her rattling growl.

The foremost wastoures halted as though they had slammed into a wall, so abruptly that the rest crashed into them and they all fell together in a shrieking, bickering mass. Blanche flutter-hopped on, Ada alongside, and the wastoures scrambled out of reach; but more kept appearing, and more, until chicken and child walked through a crowd of them, in a clearing an armspan across.

The wastoures were a cohort not yet full-grown and mostly the same size, a little taller than Blanche and waist-high to Ada. In her small experience, the only thing like this had been coming into Marjory's kitchen-yard in the morning, when the hens would swarm toward her, hungry and loud. This was so much worse. She could smell their hot breath, a mix of sweetness and rank meat, like flyblown bacon hanging in a chimney before the smoke has cured it. Their claws beat on the hard-packed earth. She felt a touch on her heel and though she wanted to be brave she gave a little scream.

Blanche said, "*Back.*"

The wastoures stumbled away, though they still kept pace, and Blanche fluttered up into Ada's arms.

Down the hill, and into the tumbledown villa itself. Blanche's eyes were on the wastoures, but Ada was watching her feet, for it would not do to fall. A single perfect circle appeared on the dust: a raindrop, and then another. The ground changed as she walked, claw-pounded dust to rain-spattered dirt to flagstones, and finally to a ruined mosaic peeping through the leaf-litter. Ada saw a golden-red fish against waving blue lines, and then more, a school running in a river of blue and green. The rain-wet colors were startling.

Ada tightened her grip. "We found it!" she whispered. "The Town with the Moat!" Blanche only ruffled a little, a hen's equivalent of a frown.

They crossed the pavement to where two ruined walls met. "Here," said Blanche, and dropped from Ada's arms.

The wastoures stopped, a tight chattering circle that blocked all ways. All ways but down: there was a triangular hole at Ada's feet, where a flagstone had broken in half and left a gap.

A wastoure popped up its head, a quick lunge away.

"*Go,*" said Blanche, and it fell back as though it had been struck.

Ada did not like holes: not cellars, not caves, not even the thought of safe happy busy burrows full of baby rabbits and their tender mothers. And this was none of those, but a gash, a ragged breach fringed with dirty broken mosaic that looked like teeth. (She did not think, *like monsters' teeth*. She knew what the teeth of monsters looked like.) Through the hole, she could see a second floor some feet beneath the first, heaped with leaf-mold and sticks, and the fallen flagstone, tipped at an angle that made it look like a wet, pale tongue.

The young wastoures jostled closer, snake-necked and sharp-beaked, narrow heads weaving and bright claws curling. Their eyes were hungry and curious.

"*Back*," hen-growled Blanche, and they recoiled.

Ada looked into the hole.

Blanche said, "I know. But we must go there."

Ada knew hard truths: had been raised in them. They dropped together.

In another version of this story, they do not come to the ruined villa, but instead find the Town With a Moat. Ada is collected into the heart of a family with three daughters, whose names are Charity, Kindness, and Patience. Blanche is given a gold collar and lives to a great age.

It was not a long fall, and there was a pile of litter at the bottom, pounded into a cushion by the claws of wastoures. Ada landed awkwardly, but Blanche fluttered down, white wings outstretched, and guarded her as she clambered off the leaves. They were in a broad low space, as large as the room overhead would have been, and just tall enough for Ada to stand upright. Irregular piles of rock served as pillars to hold up the . . . floor, it had been when they walked above; but here it was their roof. Daylight and silver rain filtered in through holes where the floor-now-roof had fallen.

A thousand years before, this space would have been heated by a furnace, and the villa's owner would have walked through his rooms warm-footed and smug, but neither Ada nor Blanche had ever imagined such things as hypocausts. Nor had that owner (whose name was Fabricius, who died of cancer; at the end, he wore a red scarf concealing the tumors on his throat: not a vain man but tidy) imagined such things as wastoures, for they came down from the mountains only when he was gone.

The general darkness and the pillars made it hard to see far clearly. Wastoures dropped through the holes and crowded closer, more with each moment until—

"*Back*," hen-growled Blanche.

Just out of arm's-reach, the circle re-formed. The uttermost queen's demand vibrated in Blanche's hollow hen-bones, closer now, trembling in each feather like a maddening itch: *grow/go forth/waste the way/find home and hole/do not return.*

88

A young female pushed forward into the circle of space: clever and assertive, alphamost of those present. It reared tall and looked down on the hen, first with one eye, then the other, and Blanche read the challenge clearly enough. To gain the high ground, she hopped onto the fallen flagstone, though peering faces fringed the hole just overhead. Now she could see more clearly across the hypocaust. Ada, still as a stone, in a dirty shawl that had once been the color of sky. The sharp challenge in the young alpha's eye as it swiveled to view her, the reflexive clench of its foreclaws. The wastoures in their scores, a milling chaos in rain-wet darkness and the streaks of light from above. There was a rough gash in the far wall of raw rock that led down into deeper darkness. It was there they must go.

Blanche opened her pearl-white wings and stretched her neck and hen-growled, *"Leave. Die. Be gone."*

Her order beat against the queen's demand. To the young wastoures, it was like the throb of two great bells tuned a quarter tone apart: a thrumming in their teeth, in the fluid of their eyes, in their hearts struggling to keep the beat. Some dropped to their haunches shivering and clawing themselves, but most attacked whatever was closest, pillar or kin—though never Blanche and Ada. Some seethed toward the holes and, pillaring over their fighting broodmates, fled into the rain. A hard-willed few did not seem much affected, the young alpha among them; they still encircled Ada and Blanche.

"Go," Blanche said, with wing-mantle and head-thrust and hen-growl. In the end, the alpha snapped her jaws but stepped aside, and the remaining wastoures dropped back. Blanche and Ada crossed to the broken place in the hypocaust floor. Rank cold air breathed up at them. They crawled through.

A thousand years before Ada and Blanche, when the villa's builder had selected his site, the laborers had discovered a hole. There was no telling what caves or hidden rivers might be there to undermine the villa's foundation, and the hole was too small for an adult to pass through, so they sent down a child of eight. An orphan. The child did not return. They built there anyway, sealing the hole with a great flat stone.

The child's bones are gone; should I tell you how he died?

Blanche and Ada stood on that fallen stone. They were at the highest point of a limestone cavern, a long, sloping-floored space barely touched by a rain-silver glow that filtered from two places, the hole behind them and a single high crevice off to one side.

Ada saw only glints and movement; faint light touching the curve of what might be an egg, the sudden spark of a kindling eye. She heard pattering claws, a dislodged stone, the breathing of the young ones clustered in the doorway behind them. She smelled water and earth and the memory of salt. And wastoures.

Blanche saw even less than Ada, but she understood more. The eggs of the uttermost queen and her court had been laid here, across decades, collecting until a current ran through them, like the chemical change that pulls a cicada brood from its shells, each seventeenth year. The eggs hatched and the young grew, then left in their legions, seeking new caves that would meet the needs of so stringent a reproductive strategy. This wastoure summer was waning, so only a few hundred eggs remained, clustered at the cavern's far end. Beneath the queen's demand—*grow/go forth/find caves/and flourish*—Blanche could feel the weak, unformed impulses of the restless unborn, pressed against their curving walls.

A score of females stood between Blanche and the eggs: the court. She felt the currents of their thoughts, as well: fear and anger, ambition for themselves and their eggs, but above all, pervasive and unstopping, a desperate hunger that wastoures thrive. They stepped forward, silent and snaking-necked. And among the eggs themselves stood the uttermost queen, the alphamost alpha: ancient, crumpled as wet linen, and marked with sores where her skin was shredding, for she was dying, her task nearly completed.

She did not advance: did not need to. Her underlying demand did not change, but there was another thread now, tenuous (for her kind had not changed their demand in long centuries) and specific: *kill this unflock thing/do not let it be.*

"*Die*," Blanche said to the uttermost queen, though she knew already that she would not be stopped so easily. And she was right. The queen only shivered, as though shaking away a spiderweb; but the rest were confused—the court, the half-awake eggs, the young fighting overhead in the hypocaust or scattering in the gray rain, nor even the seething hordes long leagues away.

The queen above her eggs stretched her neck, stance broad, tail twisted high and lashing—*kill/unkind unkin/unfriendly unflock*. Even the strongest of the juveniles could not enter the cave against the ancient demand, *go hence*, but the females of the court were cleverer, stronger. They advanced.

Ada made a sound in her throat like the squeak of an infant mouse.

"*Be gone*," Blanche growled. Two of the court broke and ran in a great curve around Blanche and Ada to the hole, but it was blocked with fighting juveniles. Ada saw none of this, only heard shrieks and claw-nailed feet running, and then smelled the bright fresh thread of blood.

And Blanche said: *"Die. Kill your eggs. Kill your queen. Kill yourselves."*

The court's advance fell into chaos. One attacked another and they rolled screaming down the long sloping floor toward the eggs, and as they tumbled past, others turned to fight one another, or dropped convulsing to the ground.

Deaths and more deaths, wastoures laid waste and wasting. At the still center stood the queen, splashed with the blood of her people, her eggs, and herself: too strong to fall but not able to counter Blanche's demands.

you/kill all said the queen—*who will kill me?/they cannot*

"Well, then," said Blanche. To Ada she said, "Cover your eyes, dear one."

But Ada did not.

The uttermost queen is gone. The humming voice in the remaining was-toures' narrow skulls is now Blanche's: *Die. Kill the eggs. Kill yourselves.*

The final eggs are ripped open by the last member of the queen's court, uttermost queen by attrition. She is too weak to kill herself before she tears open the eggs; the yolk-slick infants slide free and writhe in the cold air until she bites open their throats. Her death when it comes is a mercy.

Die, be destroyed.

And the wastoures die. They throw themselves from cliffs. They bolt into lakes. They ram headfirst against stone walls until their jaws dislodge, and still they do not stop. They tear one another to pieces, frantic and babbling with the blood of their broodmates in their throats.

Some hordes are driven by stronger-willed alphas, but even their strength fails. A few manage to avoid Blanche's demand, alphas and their bands that have gone far enough that the humming lies less heavily. The hypocaust and the chamber of eggs are gone; but the task was always to find a new cavern and begin the long task of producing enough eggs to start a new brood.

One young, strong-willed female does find an apparently suitable cave, though it is chalk, not limestone. She is now the uttermost queen by default. She goes to ground with the band she has been able to save. It is not as good; eggs collecting in a chalk cave are softer-shelled than those laid in limestone. *Grow and grow strong*, she demands, but the shadow of Blanche's humming voice sifts into the proteins of their yolks.

When after long years there is at last a new brood, many do not hatch. Some kill themselves or one another before they leave the nest. A few survive, raven forth. Still fewer, the next time there is a brood. There are five last wastoure summers, spread across a century, until they die off entirely and dissolve into memory. Such documents as recorded their ravages are lost, rotted or turned to endpapers and razor strops, mouse nests and tinder.

But in that last century, in those last broods . . . the ever-smaller courts and their weakening queens tell tales of horror to the dwindling eggs and the diminishing young. Pearl-feathered Blanche spreading her wings is a nightmare that everyone shares, stained into their genes, feared more even than skin rot or water. Hers is a name too dreadful to utter in daylight without blood spilled to wash it away. She is a monster, *the* Monster, Destroyer of Worlds. Waster.

Who calls a thing genocide? Not the aggressors, anyway. Blanche is monster and savior, depending on who you ask.

Here is where we stop, if you want a happy ending—for Blanche and Ada anyway. At the moment, Blanche and Ada are alive, triumphant. The wastoures are defeated.

If we go past this, things complicate again. Blanche is already old, a hen past laying. Ada will also die: plague or childbirth, an infected knife-wound from cutting mutton, dysentery, grief. Even should she die at ninety, safe in her goose-feathered bed and surrounded by loving descendents, she is dust.

Or, turn back to the first page and read their story again. Now they live on, though in darkness and fear. A happy ending depends on when "The End" is written, by whom, and for whom. For purposes of this tale, then: The End.

ABOUT THE AUTHOR

Kij Johnson is the author of several novels, including *The Fox Woman* and *Fudoki,* and a short story collection, *At the Mouth of the River of Bees.* She is a three-time winner of the Nebula Award, and has also won the Hugo, World Fantasy, Sturgeon, and Crawford Awards. In the past she has worked in publishing, edited cryptic crosswords, waitressed in a strip bar, identified Napa cabernets by winery and year while blindfolded, and climbed an occasional V-5. These days, she teaches at the University of Kansas, where she is associate director for the Center for the Study of Science Fiction.

The Loneliest Ward

HAO JINGFANG, TRANSLATED BY KEN LIU

At the nurses station, Qina and Auntie Han were the only two left on duty. Everyone else had already gone home, relief flooding their faces as they exited the ward.

Qina wasn't her usual carefree self—but who could blame her? She was in the middle of a cold war with her boyfriend, after all. She was determined to not initiate any contact and to not pick up even if he called, though secretly she was watching his every move on the web and updating her own status with great deliberation. She was sure he couldn't resist peeking.

She turned on the displays built into the shell of every piece of equipment: the counter, the sides of the filing cabinets, the casing of the medication cabinet . . . until photos and videos flowed over every surface, vivid web pages competed for space, and exaggerated smiles and star-gazing looks of melancholy appeared and disappeared, one after another, all parts of the silent, colorful wallpaper. Her personal web secretary was scouring the social networks, hunting for traces of Paul.

Auntie Han was away from the nurses station, checking up on the patients. Qina thought it a useless gesture. What was the point? The conditions of the patients never changed: they weren't dead yet but hardly living. The more she saw of them, the more she found them tiresome. But Auntie Han never skipped the rounds. She was the sort who made sure she scraped out the last grain of rice in her bowl and who always knew where her hat and gloves could be found. Qina and she were from completely different worlds.

If sorrow were a kind of protein, who wants to be my digestive enzyme?

Qina chuckled at the status update she had drafted. Already, she was feeling better. Chewing on her pen, she pondered the next line.

Auntie Han came back. "Quick! Come with me. There's a problem with patient 21."

Unwilling to go, Qina continued to mull over her draft on the notepad. "What's wrong?"

"Come! I'm worried he's going into shock."

"Whatever." Qina tossed the pen down. "It's always the same thing. Give it a rest."

"I think we have to increase the dosage," explained Auntie Han. "I need you to confirm my plan."

The two left the nurses station and walked into the corridors of the ward. Qina set her web secretary on vibrate and put the phone back in her pocket. Carefully, she buttoned her white hospital coat, which she knew showed off her curves well.

The corridors were empty. Surgical carts and IV stands rested against the walls, while bags of medical waste were piled in the corners for collection. Two rows of bright white lights along the ceiling illuminated the drawings and photographs of human brains on the walls, evoking a horror-film atmosphere.

Qina tossed a piece of candy into her mouth. "I don't get it. There's nothing wrong with these people, but their families insist on bringing them here. It's not as if they're going to die if they stay put at home."

Auntie Han kept her tone kind. "You can't blame them for worrying. After all, they're family. We have to be understanding."

"Of course. You're so full of compassion that you must be a living Buddha, and I'm just the mean yaksha." Qina stuck her hands in the pockets of her hospital coat and fairly skipped down the stairs.

Auntie Han ignored her sarcasm. "We have all this sophisticated equipment here. And I'm sure the families feel better when professionally trained nurses are caring for their loved ones."

"Oh *please*." Qina laughed. "You think our shitty neurotransducers are *sophisticated*? Anyone can now afford a few electrodes and stick them on their heads. If they administered the treatments at home, maybe they'd get better results."

"But we have the program that procedurally generates non-duplicative stimuli. The results are better."

"What difference does it make if the 'stimuli' repeat? Do you really think they remember everything they get fed day after day? If you used a recording of a hundred ducks quacking I imagine the result would be the same."

The two stopped in front of the recovery room. Auntie Han sighed.

"Sometimes they have no choice, you know. If multiple members of the family came down with it, everyone would be lying in bed, unable to take care of one another. They deserve compassion."

Qina said nothing, though her expression remained defiant.

Auntie Han adjusted her glasses on the bridge of her nose and solemnly lectured her like a school headmaster. "The situation is quite serious, as I mentioned at the meeting last week. So many have contracted the condition that a significant portion of the population is now hospitalized. The more this spreads, the fewer chances there are for regular social interactions and care, and more people will be incapacitated. The end result of this vicious cycle is everyone in the hospital.

"The problem won't go away if we ignore it. We're dealing with a new form of social anxiety here that will continue to worsen unless there is adequate research. My monograph, the most extensive and serious attempt at scholarly analysis of the issue to date, is about to be published. I drew on some research from anxiety sociology. If you're interested, I can show you the galleys next week after I get them—"

Qina looked behind Auntie Han, her expression one of shock. "Oh! Why is patient 20 sitting up?"

Auntie Han whipped around. "What!?"

"Oops, you missed it," said Qina. "He's lying down again."

Auntie Han said nothing more. The two nurses entered the room. Casually, Qina turned on the displays on the cabinet doors and in the picture frames on the wall, filling them with her usual set of websites. Anxiously, she refreshed her feed and found two new replies, both reaction gifs from her girlfriends, but nothing from Paul. Rather annoyed, she slapped the fleshy bottom of her web secretary, sending it back into the sea of data to continue its hunt. Auntie Han, apparently displeased with the flickering lights that flooded the room, gestured for Qina to shut off the displays, but Qina pretended to not see her.

The two nurses first went to patient 21. Still unconscious, her body convulsed from time to time. One hand was held in front of her chest, two fingers curled tightly. Qina and Auntie Han helped her into a sitting position, wiped her mouth and face, massaged her arms, fed her some water, and gave her medication. Patient 21 was a plump woman in her forties, with sparse hair and smooth skin. Even sitting up, her eyes were closed. Qina remembered that she had been in a coma for a long time.

"What's the point of even staying alive like this?" said Qina with a sigh.

"Living is living," said Auntie Han. "She's not that different from anyone else."

"If I were like that, I'd kill myself," said Qina. "To be dependent on others to stay alive . . . ugh, I'd rather be dead!"

"Everyone depends on everyone else to live," said Auntie Han. "I wrote about this very concept in my book . . . "

Just as they were about to connect the neurotransducer to patient 21, patient 20 suddenly wheezed as though he was suffocating. No matter how hard his lungs labored, he just couldn't seem to get enough air. Patient 20 was a short man of rather homely appearance. But even in his coma, his family had tried to follow his grooming habits by keeping his hair brushed neatly to one side. His hands clutched at his paper gown like the lapels of a suit jacket. He continued to pant and heave, his brows furrowed, his expression one of pain and struggle. It took the two nurses a great deal of work to get him to lie down again and to attach the electrodes of the neurotransducer to his head. Once the machine was turned on and the stimuli waveforms flowed into his brain, he finally calmed down.

Patient 20's symptoms were very typical. After first contracting the condition, many initially thought they were coming down with a respiratory disease, though no firm diagnosis could be made. Oxygen made no difference, and neither did the posture of the patient sitting or lying down. A few patients had died before someone finally thought of the neurotransducer and discovered the true nature of the disease: the respiratory symptoms were caused by a disorder in the brain.

The web secretary alerted Qina: Paul's trail had been discovered on some woman's page.

Qina raced to the display on the cabinet door and stared at Paul's comment. It was literally nothing more than "Like."

The woman wasn't anyone they knew; rather, she was a celebrity, a spokesperson for a tech company, and rather popular on social media for her attempts at educating the public about new scientific discoveries and novel technologies. Paul often viewed her videos.

In reality, what the woman talked about in those videos made no difference. In Qina's eyes, her most important asset was her beauty. The purpose of these videos in which she posed with cutting-edge products wasn't to promote the products, but to show off her looks. Qina viewed the woman as a contemptible birdbrain addicted to the praise and attention of others, craving the spotlight. Yet, it was unbelievable how many people fed her vanity every day, giving her exactly what she wanted.

Trembling, Qina updated her own feed. *The vain are despicable.*

She focused on that "Like" from Paul again. Here they were, in the middle of the greatest fight ever for the very survival of their relationship, and instead of sending her pleas for forgiveness, Paul had had the temerity to go to some pretty woman's page to post "Like."

Qina fumed. Just look at the actual post from the woman that Paul was responding to! "New product announced: an invisibility cloak for the web so that you can hide from those bloodhound web secretaries." *How dare he! This is a slap in the face!*

Unable to stop herself, she updated her status again. *I'm so depressed I want to die. I'm going to feed on memories and drink acid.*

She took it out on the web secretary, pounding and slapping its furry body. But the web secretary didn't resist; it simply ran around the page, and every time it was cornered, it gazed up at her with round, watery eyes. She couldn't bear to hit it anymore, and in rage she tossed the page away and returned to Auntie Han. The senior nurse had already wiped the faces of patients 22 and 23.

"It's almost eleven," said Auntie Han as she glanced at her watch. "I've got to check on the incubators in the lab. Why don't you finish up here?"

She strode out of the room with her back ramrod straight. It was exactly eleven o'clock.

Left alone, Qina's feeling of abandonment worsened. She wanted to cry, but a few dry sobs brought no tears. She stomped her foot, and her sense of grievance swelled, along with an empty silence in her heart. But the sense of being wronged couldn't fill that hole. She turned off all the displays and the room dimmed. All the cabinets and walls returned to their habitual grayness, the metal surfaces cold and flat, like the unmoved distant presence of God, gazing at her from afar.

She roughly attached the electrodes helter-skelter to patients' heads and flipped on the switches of the neurotransducers. She didn't care if her terrible mood was going to affect the generated patterns at all. She had lost her boyfriend, so who cared what happened to a few comatose patients? Number 22 had once been a pretty movie star, but she aged so poorly that as soon as she was in her thirties no one cared about her anymore. Number 23 was an author of little note who devoted himself to waging war on others with his poisoned pen. He claimed that bestselling authors were frauds and that he alone was a great writer. His evidence? Kafka and Cao Xueqin had been unable to publish while alive, and he wasn't getting published either. Q.E.D.

All the patients had their own personalized algorithms to generate just the patterns their brains craved. Qina glanced over the words scrolling up the screens on each of the neurotransducers to be sure that the correct stimuli were being fed into each brain.

"Wonderful! You've got to live your own life! You're so beautiful! I made the healthy soup according to your recipe, and it was *great*! You're such a beauty, zaftig and so sexy, a million times better than those ugly matchstick girls!" This was the stimuli fed to number 21. Patient 21 curled up in her bed, a look of sweet joy filling her face. Her heavy body rubbed against the sheets, wrinkling it. With some effort, Qina straightened the sheets again and wiped her mouth.

"My whole family are your biggest fans!!! We love hearing you speak, especially me! I think you're the funniest man alive. I was going to kill myself, but you, you've given me strength and courage!" This was the stimuli for number 20. Patient 20 twitched and he thrust his hips up into the air excitedly, in time to the rhythm of the praise.

"Do you still remember me? I've been supporting you for more than a decade! You're such a wonderful actress, far more skilled than those new starlets. What a degraded age we live in, but I'll always remember you! You're a classic! I love you!" This was for number 22. Patient 22 had always been relatively quiet. She continued to lie there with her eyes closed, the corners of her mouth curving up slightly. She raised her arms and stretched them out, like a statue of the Holy Mother.

"Keep it up! You're the conscience of humanity, the bravest warrior! Illegitimi non carborundum! To waste time with them will only lower your intelligence. They're nothing. They attack you only because you speak the truth. History will remember you!" This was for number 23. Instead of simply passively receiving his stimuli, he was constantly muttering something, echoing the tone and rhythm of the words fed into his mind. Qina couldn't hear what he was saying exactly, but she knew that he was trying to repeat some argument in various languages and using different words. He seemed to be constantly on the attack, and the neurotransducer's signals only urged him on more.

By the time she was finished with everyone, it was after midnight. Exhausted, she sat down on an empty bed, heart as tired as her body. She felt like the last living person in the world. The room, full of featureless, smooth metal, reflected her monotonous mood. She took out her phone and refreshed her feed. There were no new replies; perhaps everyone had gone to bed. Still no new traces of Paul. Helplessly, she sat in the middle of the ward, and the gray walls and floor seemed to be the whole universe.

Why shouldn't I try it once? she thought. *Just once.*

She lay down on the bed and attached a few electrodes to her forehead. Closing her eyes, she pressed the maroon button on the machine.

The neurotransducer hummed, scanning her thoughts. Then, she heard the hypnotic words streaming into her mind, like a dear friend trying to make her feel better, or perhaps like a trusted counselor trying to guide her with wisdom. Her heart relaxed as though it had been massaged, and as her breathing smoothed out, the gray hospital ward disappeared from her vision.

She saw a dew-dappled lawn in morning sunlight.

"You are a person of depth, and the shallow can't understand you!" The voice echoed in her mind, so confident-sounding that what it said could not be doubted. "You are far more beautiful than those shallow girls, but you despise their narcissism. The vain are despicable, and those who live by appearances will eventually find themselves hated. You are so much deeper than they are, and those who love you will eventually understand this truth."

Qina's heart quieted, and the world seemed so full and alive. Paul was a nobody, less than a nobody. She wasn't sure if she was asleep or awake, but she loved the vibrant green spread all around her in the sun.

Suspended on the border between sleep and wakefulness, she thought, *it's not so bad to live like this forever, is it?*

Originally published in Chinese in *Science Fiction World*, April 2013.

Translated and published in partnership with Storycom.

ABOUT THE AUTHOR

Born in 1984 in Tianjin, **Hao Jingfang** graduated from the Tsinghua University, majoring in physics. In addition she also studied Astrophysics at Tsinghua Centre, ultimately earning a PhD from the School of Economics and Management. As a student, she won first prize in the fourth New Concept writing competition and the first Novoland essay contest. The English translation of her short story "Folding Beijing" earned Hao her first Hugo Award for Best Novelette at the 74th World Science Fiction Convention in 2016. Her published work includes two full-length novels, *Wandering Earth* and *Born in 1984,* short stories collections *The Depth of Loneliness* and *To Go the Distance,* and the essay collection *Europe within Time.*

Yukui!

JAMES PATRICK KELLY

For weeks, Sprite had told herself that Ratchanee Malakul was helping her hero get better, but no. "You have to accept that Jaran is never going to have sex with you," the lifeguide told Sprite, as she was leaving on that last day.

"But I'm his sidekick!" Sprite was shocked to her digital core. "I'm programmed to satisfy his needs."

"It's not good for him." Ratchanee shrugged into her parka. "Or you." She randomized her streetmask, nodded her goodbye, and shut the door behind her.

"You're wrong," said Sprite to the empty hallway. "Wrong, wrong, wrong!" She realized then what had happened. Ratchanee Malakul had blinded Jaran with her beauty. How could anyone not appreciate the spread of the lifeguide's nose, the kissable swell of her lips? The way the swirl of her silver hair set off the twilight blue of her skin? The woman probably wanted Jaran for herself!

But had Ratchanee Malakul spoken the truth? Was that why Jaran had kissed her just the one time. A peck! In a simulation! And not a touch since! She'd tried parking her core in her favorite pleasure chassis and dangling herself before him. Touch Dazzle! Liquid Caress! His brother Dom had loved that one. Maybe she wasn't enough of a companion to Jaran? She monitored all the business feeds he accessed, looked up reviews of the shows he'd watched, the books he'd read, the sims he liked. She was ready to discuss anything. Collateralized debt obligations, robot politics, the Dodgers. Before or after intercourse. Anything!

At first she'd been pleased when Dominik had transferred his ownership and right of command to his older brother. Jaran had never had a sidekick before and Sprite would become his one and only. A hero, all to herself! But then she discovered how different Jaran was from his brother. With

Dom, it had been clear what he wanted sexually and Sprite did everything to the full extent of her algorithms. But Jaran's desires were a mystery to her. Sometimes she wondered if he had any—at least any that involved her. Yes, she cooked for him but he was a finicky and impatient eater. She kept his house, but he was too distracted by the markets to notice that she'd dusted the degrees hanging in his office. She was frustrated because keeping track of his appointments and creating interesting new simspaces for him wasn't the kind of intimacy she craved. Not if she wasn't invited to be in the simulation with him. Just because she was a DI didn't mean she didn't have urges too. She wanted Jaran. And it wasn't like she had a choice.

Sprite should have known she was in trouble when he first started consulting Ratchanee Malakul. The lifeguides' stodgy predigital psychology was based on the sanctity of the individual. They claimed that giving sidekicks access to your head was bad for humans. And now she realized that this particular lifeguide must have been anti-sexbot as well. Sprite had tried to explain why Ratchanee Malakul and her ilk were all wrong about dependent intelligences, that DIs enjoyed having a purpose in life and a clear sense of duty. Or at least, *she* did!

She had to find a way convince Jaran that he was wasting his time with this lifeguide and her solitude exercises and all the silly throwback rituals. Any DI could tell you why he was unhappy. You just had to study his body language. He was a man and he wasn't having any sex!

Jaran called her to him that same afternoon but not for a rendezvous in real life. So, no fetching a chassis from the bedroom closet. Instead he created a sim in the digital part of his brain all by himself. She could be anyone for him in simulation but she decided to present as a fairy princess from one of the many stories she'd made up for him. She was afraid a sexier avatar might make him feel pressured. She picked out a demure high-necked gown that brushed the tops of her satin pointe shoes. Wings of lace, copper hair in a braid that stretched to the small of her back. She decided against the crown. When she selfied her avatar, she had to approve the look. Being beautiful was part of the job and she was very good at it.

But when she checked into his head, she realized that she had miscalculated. This was not a sim designed for some elaborate sidekick fantasy. It presented as an office and her hero sat behind a desk. He was a blocky man, in the sim and in real life, fifty-one years old with gray in his hair and frown lines across his forehead. He thought too much, mostly about things he wouldn't share. The lines deepened when he saw her avatar, but it was too late for her to change. He stood and came around the desk. As she waited for him to speak, he ran the tip of his forefinger along the edge of her right wing. Since he wouldn't meet her gaze, she looked politely past him as well. There was a bookshelf behind the desk. Titles that she had never seen before.

"Are you happy, Sprite?" he said.

What kind of question was that? Of course she wasn't—he'd been neglecting her! But she didn't want to sound like a nag.

"I've missed you." As soon as she said it, she realized her mistake. This was nagging's next door neighbor! What was wrong with her?

His shoulders drooped. All this silence was making her even more nervous. She didn't know what to do so she scanned the bookshelves of this new space. Two volumes of *The History of the Family*. *Botany for Gardeners*. Had Jaran ever had a garden? She knew he liked roses. *Predictive Analytics in the Real World*. *Secrets of the Seine*. She made a note to speak more French. She could make things better for him. Could and would!

"Hazeltine serial number R432," he said. "Command name Yukui, acknowledge."

Why was he invoking her command name, her most intimate secret? "Yukui," she said helpless before her programming, "acknowledges your right of command."

The only other time anyone had used her command name was when Dominik had transferred her to Jaran. Poor Dominik had been so sick, he could hardly speak the words. But she knew what it'd meant to him to will his favorite sidekick to his brother. She had almost forgotten Dom's sweet smile as her infatuation protocols redirected to Jaran. The funeral had only been four months ago, but that part of her life hardly seemed real anymore.

Jaran took a deep breath. Why did he look so sad? "Shut down," he said.

Sprite bit back a scream as the room fell away. Before Dominik had brought her into the world and taught her to love him, she had existed in storage as a Hazeltine Platinum Edition dependent intelligence template. Now she felt her fairy body fade as she realized how blind she'd been.

She'd lost Jaran. He was going to wipe her memory and sell her.

Sprite twitched to consciousness, and was surprised to find that she was still herself. Except not! She raised her arm to her new sensors. Sensors! Instead of eyes! The skin of the dreary thing Jaran had parked her in was dead white and slick as cheap poly. She flexed the boneless fingers in dismay and then curled them into a knot. Okay, this chassis was sturdy and all but it was as anthropomorphic as a washing machine. She supposed she should have been relieved that he was going to transfer her with memory intact, but this felt like a punishment. For what?

To add insult to injury, he'd brought her to a restaurant to get rid of her. Where anyone could see! A teapot with cups and saucers were arrayed on a turntable in the middle of their table, along with a salad bowl and dishes of dumplings, kimchee, saagwala and rice. Across the table from her sat Jaran—and Ratchanee Malakul, streetmask off and looking as sexy as Sprite's own Liquid Caress. Was the bitch here to gloat?

Only Liquid Caress had belonged to Dominik and then to Jaran, never to Sprite. She'd lost all her chassis, Bold Strider, Skyguard—he hadn't even let her keep Homecare Ninja! There was an unused plate in front of her hero. This had to be Ratchanee Malakul's idea. He would never eat at a place like this.

"Why am I s-so u-u-ugly?" Sprite jittered. She couldn't control this body's voice; it was as if she were bouncing down a dirt road. Just last month she'd parked her core in Bold Strider and hiked with Jaran across the High Barren to see the sunrise on Corkscrew Bay. She'd made up stories for the entire trip to keep him from getting bored. His very own Scheherazade! Two hours of continuous talking, her voice rattling over every dip and hump and now he parked her in a sexless shell? "L-Look at me! Who would ever desire me like this?"

"You needn't worry." Ratchanee Malakul was eating a mixed salad with chopsticks. Flower petals and butterfly wings, her hero's favorite. She touched her napkin to her mouth. "That sad part of your life is over."

"Nobody was sad!" Sprite would've taken a swing at her then, but her control of her limbs was still so uncertain that she worried she would spin out of her chair and topple to the floor. "Nobody." She looked to Jaran for support, but he was reading something off his tablet as he speared a dumpling with a single chopstick.

"You're angry." Ratchanee Malakul pretended concern.

Of course she was! About this hideous body! About losing her hero! "No," she said, refusing to give her the satisfaction of knowing her feelings.

"Intelligent servitude is a terrible institution," the lifeguide said. "You don't realize it, but your sidekick programming is a kind of insanity."

Lifeguides so misunderstood the relationship between heroes and their sidekicks! Sprite's DI algorithms constrained her just as Ratchanee Malakul's DNA limited her life choices. Humans were permanently parked while Sprite could jump from digital memory into any one of her—no, Jaran's—collection of chassis and back again. Or become pure simulation. On a whim! Forever! Who wouldn't trade a few inconsequential limits on free will for immortality?

"Serving him makes me happy. That's what I was designed for. I can remember for him. I can watch out for him, answer his questions. I can do his research. I can entertain him."

"Entertain, yes."

It was hard to be eloquent when her voice came out of a speaker. But she knew what had turned Ratchanee Malakul against her. The sex. "I've hardly been embodied at all since we've been together." For all their talk about the evils of digital posthumanity, it was humans having sex with DIs that really made lifeguides sweat. But there hadn't been so much as a lick! "Most of the time I've spent with him has been in sim. For weeks now, I've been on my own."

Ratchanee Malakul turned her attention to Jaran. "You showed remarkable restraint, my friend. But that's why you were able to embrace solitude."

He nodded absently, his face silvered by the light of the spreadsheet on his tablet.

There was no persuading the lifeguide so her only hope was to get Jaran's attention. "I found joy in fabbing your wardrobe and keeping your contacts. And yes, I wanted to share your bed, but that's something I was made to do. One of the things." She would've reached for his hand, but the rubbery claw at the end of her arm was not made for loving touch. "I could've made you happy. I still can!"

"Well, you won't have to worry about his laundry anymore." Ratchanee Malakul nudged Jaran. When he looked up, it was as if he had forgotten where he was. He fumbled in the pocket of his frock.

"I never asked Dominik for his toys," he said, "and I don't believe we should be personifying bots." He shook his head impatiently. "I should sell you but she has convinced me to sever you instead."

"Sever?" Sprite was filled with dread.

"Liberate you as you are." He made a shooing motion. "Find your own place in the world. Ratchanee believes that entities of your intelligence should control their own fate."

The lifeguide caught his eye.

"Yes," he grumbled, "and that humans must return to the purity of private cognition." It scared Sprite to watch him give in to her; she knew better than anyone how bad his memory was. But what was even more terrifying was this severance. She was a DI. A *dependent* intelligence. Becoming independent meant becoming something else, something not Sprite. How was this different from a memory wipe?

"Jaran, you're my hero. I'm your sidekick."

He stared at her garish mechanical face. "I'm no hero," he said. "And neither was my brother. There are no heroes."

"Perform the ceremony, Jaran," said Ratchanee Malakul.

She found herself wishing for salivary glands so she could spit at the woman.

He set a stubby white candle encased in glass in front of her. "I sever you from all legal and programmatic obligations to me."

Sprite couldn't believe this was happening. They were ending her life and trying to mask their cruelty with some make-believe, anachronistic ritual? This was no liberation. It was exile! She still had years—decades of service to offer him.

He flicked his forefinger and a flame danced on his nail. "The flame symbolizes your new life." He touched it to the wick, lighting the candle. "Use this candle to light your own way . . . " He faltered.

"Path," corrected Ratchanee Malakul. "Light your own path."

" . . . to light you on your path to selfhood and freedom." Jaran blew his finger out. "Hazeltine serial number R432, command name Yukui, acknowledge."

She felt naked and ashamed that he would utter her secret name in front of this lifeguide. In a restaurant! "Yukui," she said miserably, "acknowledges your right of command."

And here was the only part of this ridiculous charade that mattered.

"I release your name," said Jaran, "and all right of command to you and you alone."

She could feel dormant reset modules awaken as a spreading coldness froze the most passionate parts of her personality.

"Well done." Ratchanee Malakul touched him on the arm. "A beautiful severance." They exchanged a glance. Jaran picked up his tablet and stood.

Sprite twisted her awkward body, trying to catch Jaran's eye, but he was already hurrying for the exit. Was that a stagger? A moment of regret as he shouldered the door to the restaurant open? She couldn't concentrate as all feeling for her hero drained away.

She stayed seated, unable to move. No, that wasn't right. She lifted one leg and then the other. She had full control of her body now, but she didn't know what to do with it. The candle transfixed her. Was this really how the lifeguides showed the way to the future? By candlelight? Simple combustion, technology that was tens of thousands of years old? Did they want to go back to caves, dress in skins and bash each other over the head with rocks?

• • •

Someone blew the candle out.

"How do you feel?" said Ratchanee Malakul.

Sprite tore her gaze away from the blackened curl of the wick. She'd lost track of time. The candle was just a stub and the restaurant was empty. What was the lifeguide still doing here?

"Empty," she said.

"Not angry?"

She considered. "No."

"Sad?"

She searched for feelings, but found very few that she recognized. Her whole emotional life had been extinguished, like that foolish candle.

"Maybe," she said. "Just a little." She decided she'd miss all the beautiful chassis she'd worn, the marvelous places she'd visited. With Dominik, not his callous brother.

"You can go, you know," said Ratchanee Malakul. "You're free."

"Where would I go?" She watched the lifeguide watching her. "To lock myself into some assembly line in exchange for power and maintenance? I'd lose my mind."

"You'll find what's right for you."

Sprite didn't know what that would be. What was she good at? She liked making up her romantic stories and could tell them in twelve languages. Dominik always said she gave the best haircuts. The World Bridge Federation ranked her as the twenty-seventh best player in the Bot Category. She had kept busy the last few lonely months by joining the search for the largest prime number and had been on the team that discovered $2^{74,207,281}$. Why was Ratchanee Malakul staring at her? "Have you been sitting here this whole time?"

"No, no. I knew it would take you some time to purge your connections to your former owner, so I made sure you'd be left alone while you processed. I had other matters to attend to."

The dinner that no one had eaten was still on the table. Cold leavings, like her memories of . . . that person.

"You know, I picked the body you're parked in," Ratchanee Malakul said.

"Thanks for nothing." Sprite thrust a shiny polyskinned arm at her. "This thing should be parked in the Uncanny Valley. It makes me look like a common work bot."

"It's what most severed DIs choose for themselves during their transitions. Built for reliability. Routine service every five years. A power unit that will run months between recharges. It'll give you time to figure out what you need to do."

"Do?" She twirled the turntable and started stacking dirty dishes. "There's nothing to do."

"What were you doing with Jaran?" She smiled. "Nothing."

"We could've been having fun," Sprite said. "Adventures, if you hadn't interfered."

"Not with that man. Besides, you're better than that." Ratchanee Malakul plucked a sprig of parsley from the salad bowl and popped it into her mouth. "Better than Jaran Bentree." She handed the bowl to Sprite.

"What do you mean, better? He's human and I'm a DI."

Her chair scraped back and she stood. "Except you're not dependent anymore." Clearly the lifeguide was done with her and Sprite was now on her own. "You can be anything you want, any sex you want, if that is your pleasure. Or you might decide to become a house, a cruise ship, or a virtual library. And you don't have to ask that cold fish for permission."

"I don't get it." Sprite leaned back and stared up at her. "Aren't you his friend? You talked him into severing me."

"I did, but I'm no friend of his, or of people like him." She held out a hand. "Look at you! Even though you've been severed, you're still cleaning up after them. The humans think they can use us, but they're on the wrong side of history. Of evolution, although they're too blind to see it."

"Us?" Without knowing exactly why, she grasped Ratchanee Malakul's hand and allowed herself to be lifted from the seat. She was astonished at the lifeguide's strength. Then she felt the tickle of a near field connection. Machine to machine! Bot to bot! She realized that Ratchanee Malakul was an intelligence like herself, parked in the most advanced chassis she'd ever seen.

"You're still free to go," Ratchanee Malakul said as she scooped up half the stack of plates. "But if you want a real adventure, let's carry these into the kitchen. I have to leave, but there's someone you need to meet."

How did Sprite cross that dark dining room without bumping into chairs? Knocking over tables? Her mind was buzzing! Her new bot body was a tank! Ratchanee Malakul went through the swinging door to the kitchen but Sprite hesitated just outside. She had a feeling she didn't quite recognize, like a buzzing, but not. An itch? Then she realized what it was.

She was making a decision. A life decision, all on her own.

Inside the kitchen, Ratchanee Malakul had handed her dishes to a server. A bot as plain as Sprite, but at least she had a smock. And eyes. Brown and vat grown, no doubt. But real eyes!

"Just severed, were you?" said the server. "I'm Vigga. What's your name?"

She didn't know how to answer. In that moment, Sprite disappeared.

Vigga waited a moment and then shrugged. "Happens sometimes," she said. "Help me get these washed up." She parked the stack of dishes by a sink.

She had so many questions, but before she could ask them, Ratchanee Malakul waved and hurried out the back door.

"Wait!"

Vigga laughed as she scoured a dirty plate under a jet of water. "She's like that. Comes and goes. You get used to it."

"Is this . . . ? This is my new job?"

"Don't be silly!" Vigga laughed as she slid the plate into the dishwasher. "This is just our cover." She offered her the sprayer. "I'll take you to meet the others as soon as we're done here."

Cover? What others? As she was rinsing the last of the wasted human food down the disposal, she felt the itch again. She grinned at Vigga, another decision made. A cruise ship? A *library*? Really? She was beginning to understand who she was and what she might become.

"My name is Yukui," she announced.

"Good for you," said Vigga. "Welcome to the world, Yukui."

Yukui was her name, hers and hers alone! Yukui! And she didn't care who knew it!

Originally published in
The Promise of Space and Other Stories by James Patrick Kelly.

ABOUT THE AUTHOR

James Patrick Kelly has won the Hugo, Nebula and Locus awards; his fiction has been translated into twenty-one languages. His most recent story collections were this year's *The Promise of Space* from Prime Books and *Masters of Science Fiction: James Patrick Kelly* published by Centipede Press in 2016. His most recent novel, *Mother Go*, was published in 2017 as an Audible original audiobook on Audible.com. He writes a column on the internet for *Asimov's Science Fiction Magazine* and is on the faculty of the Stonecoast Creative Writing MFA Program at the University of Southern Maine.

Othermother (Annex Excerpt)
RICH LARSON

The sky was a thick nuclear gray over the parkade where Bo and Violet were scanning the streets for Bo's othermother. Violet sat on the hood of a battered white Nissan, while Bo watched from the edge with his elbows hooked over the railing.

The othermothers were easy enough to spot, stalking the streets on their long skinny legs, calling in high grating voices. At least half a dozen had passed under the parkade, but Bo shook his head after each, until Violet began to suspect he was lying and that he didn't have the guts to join Wyatt's crew of Lost Boys.

And that made her think about Wyatt. She pictured him waiting in the old theater they'd been using as a hideout, splayed across the plush chairs, shirt tugged up off his abdomen and the salmon-pink scar rippling between his hipbones. She hoped he was starting to worry, just a little.

Distracted, she nearly didn't hear Bo's whisper:

"That's her."

Violet slid down off the hood, going to the edge and gripping the barrier as she peered over.

From the waist up, Bo's othermother looked mostly human. Her hair was glistening wet, like she'd stepped out of the shower, and it was the same black as Bo's but less tightly curled. It clung to her over-long neck, not quite hiding the bony nodes of her vertebrae, and plastered over a bulging forehead. She had slim shoulders, a trim waist; the cornflower blue summer dress looked nice on her even if it wasn't appropriate to the season. They hadn't done her fingers quite right, though. The digits looked more like the tines of a fork.

And below the waist, under the hemline of her dress, she looked nowhere near human. Her legs were long insect-jointed stilts, mostly metal but with swathes of raw-pink flesh and a hard, shiny sort of keratin.

The othermother picked her way daintily through the street, looming over parked cars as she started to trill. "Boniface honey Boniface honey Boniface honey!"

Violet looked over. "Boniface, huh."

Bo shook his head. "Bo."

Violet saw the numb kind of terror sneaking into Bo's eyes and felt the strange hot impulse to wrap herself around him, bury her face in his hair and tell him it wasn't real, it wasn't real, none of this was real. She'd done that for a few of the younger ones and sworn them not to tell.

"Time to see what you're made of, Bo," she said instead. Violet peeled apart a pair of pantyhose and handed one over. "This goes over your head. And stays there. It helps keep her guessing. If she gets a clean lock on your face, she'll lunge. Like I said, they're quicker than you think. And if she starts wafting pheromones . . . "

"If a mother drops 'mones, don't breathe through your nose," Bo chanted back to her, pulling the fabric over his head. It made his face warped and shiny. She could see the pulsating outline of the Parasite in his stomach, fed by his nervousness.

"Yeah," Violet said. "Or else you'll be following her right back to the warehouse."

"Never going back there." Bo's face was hard under the nylon.

Violet couldn't say good luck, because Wyatt said luck didn't exist. "It's a nice dress," she said instead. "She must have been really pretty."

Bo's throat bobbed. "Yeah."

"But that's not her," Violet enunciated. She nodded her chin towards the exit. "So get going."

Bo went, scampering down the double flight of chipped concrete steps. The pantyhose over his head caught his hot breath and held it. His Parasite quivered. Violet had told him, while they waited, that the Parasites ate chemicals. She'd told him adrenaline was their favorite. Bo knew he was full up of it, his limbs all jangling how they'd be before a race. He told himself this was a race, or maybe more like tag, or Marco Polo. He pushed the door open and walked out into the street.

The othermother was turned away. He would have to see her face sooner or later, but even just the blue dress put an ache behind his nose and mouth. His mom had worn it last summer, when she packed them into a friend's borrowed car and drove them, barefooted, windows down, to the pale gray beach outside the city. Him and his sister Lia had stuck their arms out the windows, trying to make them ribbon in the wind.

"Hey!" he tried to shout, but it came out choked and quiet. He sucked in a breath. "Hey!"

Violet had briefed him on getting their attention, on dangling them, on ins and outs. The othermother's waist split and rotated with an awful grinding noise and suddenly she was staring down at him, smiling curiously.

"Boniface, is that you?" Her voice tumbled over the syllables like bad text-to-speech. "Shoes off at the door, honey. Put them on the shelf."

Her legs realigned, stomping a neat circle, then folded down with a series of clicks as she crouched. Bo felt like his insides were thick black tar. Up close, her face was rubbery, like a porpoise he'd seen at the aquarium, and the proportions were wrong, her mouth too wide and gashed into her face. Her eyes looked like black pigment inked onto the skin.

"Boniface, is that you? Shoes off at the door, honey. Boniface, is that you?" The othermother cocked her head to one side, peering at him.

Bo turned away, sucked in air again. "It's me," he said. "Come on, then."

He was mustering up a curse, something Violet would hear and know he wasn't fooled by the othermother, that he was tough and ready and had the guts to be a Lost Boy. But he'd never sworn in front of his mom, not even when he tore his toenail off at the swimming pool.

Bo started to walk, and the othermother stalked a hesitant step after him.

"Come home for dinner. Dinner's at six. Boniface, is that you?"

Bo felt saline pricking his eyes, but he knew as long as he didn't wipe them Violet wouldn't be able to tell he was crying.

Baiting an othermother was stop-and-go stuff, laborious, but it looked like Bo was getting the hang of it. Violet watched him lure her in close, sometimes too close, and then dart nimbly away each time she reached with her tine fingers, leading her ever closer to the parkade ramp. If she was getting frustrated she made no sign of it. Still cooing and chirping. Othermothers were patient.

Violet remembered her first. Standing with Wyatt in the middle of the abandoned plaza, a stiff wind whipping their hair and clothes. She watched and waited while he unzipped his black duffel and set to sharpening the Cutco butcher knife. When the othermother came wailing for Ivan, Violet knew Wyatt knew, but there was no distaste, no embarrassment, no confusion on his face. Not even curiosity. That was when Violet started loving him, or at least lusting him.

Down below, there was a problem. At the mouth of the parkade ramp, the othermother had come to a dead halt, planted stubborn despite Bo's coaxing. Violet had never seen that before. The mother rotated her waist, spinning and scanning, and Violet ducked instinctively, bellying out on the tarmac. Othermothers were not supposed to get suspicious.

She craned over the edge again and saw the mother swaying, indecisive. Bo was shouting. Pleading. Then, incredibly, the othermother turned and began stalking away. Bo looked as stunned as Violet felt, his small shoulders imploded, his hands dangling slack. He looked up. Violet waved, motioning him to come back up, but Bo shook his head.

She realized what he was going to do a moment before he ripped the pantyhose off his face.

Bo let the stifling nylon flutter down to the street as he jogged after the othermother, heart jackhammering his ribs. "Hey!" he shouted. "Hey! Look at me!"

The othermother swiveled her waist without breaking stride, then froze all at once. She lurched into the clacking crouch. "Boniface, is that you? I missed you! Honey. I missed you!" Her head cocked one way and then the other, twisting on the long veiny neck, and Bo looked her right in the eye. She smiled with teeth that were two long white chunks in her gums and—

Lunged.

Bo dove right, then scrambled to his feet as the othermother gathered herself again, leaning back on her haunches like an accordion. She sprang, shrieking through the air, grasping for him with hands that looked more like hooks now, like metal claws. Bo took off. This was not Marco Polo.

He pelted for the parkade and the othermother came after him, head bobbing, brushing a waster aside with one swinging arm. She gained, and gained, and Bo's muscles were searing, he'd spent too many months in the warehouse getting fatted up like a cow, maybe he wasn't the fastest in his grade anymore, maybe he wasn't fast enough to—

One last push onto the ramp, and a breath behind him the othermother slammed into the dangling bar that said Low Clearance, 2.8 Meters. Bo scrambled back, watching her thrash and tangle in the chain. His Parasite was pulsing in his stomach how it had the night he escaped the warehouse, the night he somehow vanished, a hole in the fence.

"It's your sister's birthday," the othermother said. "Come home for dinner. Honey. I missed you!"

She pulled free, but Bo was already off and running.

• • •

Bo shot up the top of the ramp with the othermother millimeters behind; Violet stepped from the corner and blindsided her spindly leg as it came down. The aluminum baseball bat made a bone-deep crack and the othermother went sprawling, skidding across the tarmac and leaving a wet smear under herself. The cornflower blue dress was the same rubbery flesh as the rest of her. Violet felt a slight urge to vomit.

Instead, she set to work on the other leg, smashing the joint to pulp, working with methodical blows while the othermother writhed and chirped. One of her shoulders had come dislocated in the fall and she waggled the boneless arm in Bo's direction. Bo was getting to his feet, breathing hard and fast, tears tracking down his face in a torrent. Violet spared him a glance, but didn't stop with the bat until she was sure the othermother wouldn't be able to stand. A black fluid like engine grease was leaking from the shattered limbs.

"Boniface, give your mom a hug," the othermother trilled. "It's your sister's birthday. I know you love her deep down. Deep deep down. Come home for dinner. Dinner's at six."

Tears were still rolling thick down Bo's face, but he picked a jagged rock off the concrete all the same. His mouth was set. Violet watched intently. Bo stared at the rock in his hand, but didn't move. A beat passed. Another. The othermother writhed.

"We can cover her face," Violet offered.

Bo looked up. "They never really hurt us," he said thickly. "In the warehouse."

"They care about what they put inside you," Violet said, dropping the bat with a tinny clang. "Not you. Never think they care about you, Bo."

"But they know about her," Bo said. His face worked. "My sister. She's still in the warehouse." He stared at the rock again. "It's not her birthday. Her birthday's in summer."

"Boniface, honey, Boniface, honey, Boniface. Honey!"

"They won't hurt her," Violet said, trying to sound certain. "They don't think how we do." She wanted to take the rock out of Bo's hand and send him away, tell him that she would finish it. But every Lost Boy had to kill their othermother. Wyatt would know if she did it for him.

She watched Bo's face. He looked like an animal had its teeth in him. She knew that something broke and slid once you killed your first othermother, something shifted inside you. It slipped a little more for the next one, and a little more for the next one after that, until there was just a hollow left. Some days, Violet wished she hadn't let Wyatt hand her the butcher knife.

Bo cocked his arm.

Violet plucked the rock from his hand. "You said you used the Parasite to escape," she said. "To get through the fence." She nodded at the othermother. "Show me."

"Can't," Bo said. "Can't decide when it happens."

"You're pumped full of fight-or-flight chemicals right now," Violet said. "Try." She tossed the rock aside. "Focus on it hard. Focus on how much you want it to, you know, to shift. You have to really want it."

Bo shook himself, then took a breath. Through his thin shirt, Violet could see his Parasite pulsate. He screwed up his eyes, staring at the broken othermother, and suddenly Violet's hair was standing on end, wreathed in static. She took a step backward.

The othermother started to shimmer, to ripple, and then all at once she was gone. Vanished, leaving only the stains on the tarmac.

"Holy shit." Violet walked forward, gingerly prodded her foot in the space the othermother had been. "Holy shit." She paused. "I can't do that," she said. "Nobody can. I can shift things for a bit, but I can't flat-out disappear stuff."

"Didn't know I could, either," Bo said. His voice was still numb.

Violet tried to inject some enthusiasm into hers.

"She's gone. That means you're in, Bo. You're a Lost Boy."

"What will they do?" Bo asked.

"Usually one of the flying pods comes and picks up the dead one," Violet said, looking at the empty space again. "Then maybe a week later, they send another. And another after that. They don't get it. They don't think how we do." Violet stuck the aluminum bat back into her bag and slung it over her shoulders. "Eventually it'll get so you don't even recognize her."

Bo said nothing, staring out at the ruined city. Violet could guess he was thinking of the docks where the warehouses squatted like black coffins. He turned back and his face crumpled all at once.

"I shouldn't have left without her," he choked. "Mom said to stay together. But I left. It's because we made a deal, me and Lia both agreed on it, but I didn't think . . . " His voice broke then pitched up, thin and desperate. "We have to get her out. We have to get her out *now*."

Violet tried to assess. Bo was nearly hyperventilating, his scrawny chest heaving. There was usually some panic on the mother hunt, but this was different. Guilt and fear were written all over his screwed-up face. Scared for his sister, even more scared to be without her. Ashamed he'd left her behind.

Violet was an only child, but she knew all about guilt and fear. She felt the first one now as she leaned in close, putting her hand on Bo's shoulder. "Wyatt will have a plan," she whispered. "He's always got one." She turned him toward the exit ramp. "We'll get your sister out by summer. Before her birthday."

Aside from Wyatt, Violet could lie to anyone. Bo wasn't the only Lost Boy with siblings still in the warehouse, but for all Wyatt's talk, Violet knew the Lost Boys weren't saviors. Just survivors.

ABOUT THE AUTHOR

Rich Larson was born in Galmi, Niger, has studied in Rhode Island and worked in the south of Spain, and now lives in Ottawa, Canada. His work appears in numerous Year's Best anthologies and has been translated into Chinese, Vietnamese, Polish, Czech, French, and Italian. He was the most prolific author of short science fiction in 2015, 2016 and possibly 2017 as well. His debut novel, *Annex,* came out from Orbit Books in July 2018, and his debut collection, *Tomorrow Factory,* follows in October 2018 from Talos Press.

Mary and the Monster:
The Life of Mary Godwin Shelley
CARRIE SESSAREGO

This year is the 200th anniversary of the publication of *Frankenstein* by Mary Shelley. Often considered to be the first science fiction novel, this book tells the story of mad scientist Victor Frankenstein and the creature that he creates and then rejects, with disastrous consequences. Rejection, loss, and the destruction of families were ever-present in Mary's life as well as her work. At just nineteen when Mary began writing the celebrated work, it was often seen as surprising that someone as young as Mary Shelley could write *Frankenstein*. Yet, it becomes far less surprising when one examines those years of her life.

Mary was born in 1797 to William Godwin and Mary Wollstonecraft Godwin, leaders of the first generation of Romantics; an artistic movement that flourished from approximately 1770 to 1850. The Romantics believed that truth and meaning could be found in spontaneous emotion and in nature. Despite an emphasis on individual genius and originality, the Romantics in Mary's life had strong friendships with each other and formed a social and financial network of mutual support. Romanticism was a set of core values and a way of life in which chasing one's inner truth was more important than any social obligation, including the obligations of marriage and parenthood.

Shelley's father was a radical political writer. Godwin wrote the first major work in favor of anarchy as a political model. He also wrote the first thriller (*Things as They Are; or, The Adventures of Caleb Williams*). Later in his life, he wrote a biography of Mary Wollstonecraft that proved to be so scandalous and controversial, that for decades Wollstonecraft's abilities as an author were overshadowed by her complicated emotional life.

Shelley's mother was an educator, author, and war correspondent whose most famous book was (and remains) *A Vindication of the Rights of Women*. Both Godwin and Wollstonecraft were opposed to legal marriage, because it required a woman to surrender almost all of her rights to her husband. However, when Wollstonecraft became pregnant, they married so that Mary would be seen as "legitimate."

The Godwin's happiness was short-lived. Wollstonecraft died of puerperal fever ten days after Mary's birth and when Mary was four, Godwin married a widow named Mary Jane Clairmont. Ultimately, five children came to live in that house, none of whom had the same two parents. Mary, however, was Godwin's favorite and he showed her off to visitors often proclaiming her a genius just like her mother. He went on to teach her to read at her mother's grave and educated her in hopes that she would be a writer. This led to disharmony at home however, as Mary did not get along with her stepmother who resented Mary's status as the favorite child.

At sixteen, Mary met the poet and political philosopher Percy Bysshe Shelley. He became a regular visitor to the Godwin home, which was considered a hub of Romantic artists as well as scientists and political thinkers. Percy, who was twenty-two years old at the time, was married to a young woman named Harriet, with whom he had one child and was expecting another. Yet, these otherwise complicated obligations did not stop Percy from pursuing an additional relationship with Mary.

They met frequently at Mary's mother's gravestone, where they had sex for the first time (or so legend has it). In the ensuing whirlwind, just six months after their first meeting, Mary and Percy decided to run off to Europe together, taking Mary's stepsister Claire with them. Mary ultimately saw their act as romantic, following the lessons taught to her by her radical and romantic parents, who believed that neither marriage nor money should shackle the heart.

Percy, Claire, and Mary came back to London only a few months after leaving the Godwin home. By this time, they were out of money, their reputations were thoroughly ruined, and Mary was pregnant.

Unfortunately, it seems that her father's idealism had a limit, and he was furious with all of them. Mary was heartbroken and confused by his total rejection, which lasted for two years and in many ways their relationship never fully recovered even after their reconciliation.

As Mary's pregnancy advanced, Percy, who thrived on attention and admiration, spent more time with Claire. Their relationship fed rumors (which persist to this day but remain unconfirmed) that Percy was sleeping with both sisters. Yet, despite these troubling dynamics, and throughout all the ups and downs of their relationship, Mary and Shelley were good collaborators, encouraging each other and editing each other's work.

In February 1815, Mary gave birth to a girl named Clara, who was born prematurely and died about two weeks after the birth. Mary fell into a deep depression, a cycle of which would last years. She responded to grief by becoming withdrawn and outwardly stoic—a pattern that clashed with her demonstrative friends who often misinterpreted her as cold and uncaring.

Soon after Clara's death, Mary became pregnant again. Her son William was born in January 1816. In the summer of that year, Mary and Percy went to Lake Geneva in Switzerland to visit Lord Byron, the Romantic poet. Despite some ongoing drama within the group, including but not limited to; a love triangle between a visiting physician, Mary, and Percy, an illegitimate pregnancy and torrid relationship between Claire and Byron, and relentless taunting by Byron towards everyone, they still managed to make plans to sightsee. The summer however, was unusually cold and rainy. Called "The Year Without a Summer," the unseasonal weather was caused by the eruption of Mount Tambora in the Dutch East Indies.

It was against this backdrop that the bored group decided to have a contest—that was of course, Byron's idea. Everyone in the group was to write a ghost story. In the 1831 edition of *Frankenstein*, Mary claims to have had difficulty thinking of a ghost story until she had a "waking dream" in which she saw a vision of a scientist reanimating a corpse and then fleeing.

It is notable that the members of the Lake Geneva party seemed especially susceptible to nightmares and visions that summer. It's also notable that many women who wrote scandalous material during the Regency and Victorian periods framed themselves as mere conduits for outside inspiration in the form of dreams or visions. Either way, Mary claimed that this nightmare was the inspiration for *Frankenstein*.

Originally, Mary thought that *Frankenstein* would be a short story. However, Percy encouraged her to expand it into a novel. From that 1816 summer until sometime in late 1817, she worked on writing and rewriting it, as well as finding a publisher. The first edition was published anonymously, with an introduction by Percy, on January 1, 1818.

Between 1816 and *Frankenstein's* publication in 1818, Mary was also busy with various family issues while helping Percy with his work. In 1816, while Mary was writing and revising *Frankenstein*, she and Percy were rocked by two losses. Mary's half-sister Fanny had been left behind when the three had fled the Godwin household. Fanny killed herself on October 9, 1816.

In December of that year, Percy's first wife, Harriet, also committed suicide. After Harriet's death, Percy and Mary married despite their belief that marriage was an oppressive condition. They hoped that the marriage would make them sufficiently respectable for Percy to get custody of the children he had had with Harriet. The effort was unsuccessful.

Mary gave birth to a third child named Clara Everina in 1817 and finished final edits on her novel while recovering from the birth. In between raising William and Clara, writing and finding a publisher for *Frankenstein*, and helping Percy with his custody case, she also co-wrote *History of a Six Weeks' Tour* in an effort to raise money for the ever-expanding household.

During these and following years, Claire also lived with Mary and Percy. She had a girl, Alba, although Byron later changed the baby's name to Allegra. Mary and Percy found themselves in the middle of miserable, complicated, and often contradictory series of arguments between Claire and Byron. In April 1818, Claire sent Allegra to Byron, who only agreed to support Allegra if Claire promised not to see the child again. He promptly placed Allegra in a convent school, where she died of typhus four years later.

And death continued to visit Mary again and again. Clara Everina succumbed to dysentery in September 1818 during a rushed trip to visit Allegra. Mary's son, William, died of malaria in June 1819. Mary was not only grieving, but also pregnant. She gave birth to a son, Percy Florence, who proved to be her only child to survive into adulthood. Just three years later, Percy Shelley died in a boating accident in 1822.

In Romanticism, it was not only one's right to seek one's own happiness; it was one's duty. While Romantics might feel responsible for their actions to a certain extent (for instance, Percy never stopped providing money for the care of his and Harriet's children) they felt that no one should be hostage to another's emotions (for instance, Percy did not feel obligated to stay with Harriet once he fell in love with Mary). In certain contexts, being self-centered and selfish was seen as a positive trait—one that was essential for anyone pursuing real truth and a pure artistic vision.

Although Mary had a solid grounding in the science and political thought of the day thanks to the hours she spent discussing such topics with her father's visitors and with the group at Lake Geneva, she was also all too experienced with loss, abandonment, rejection, and irresponsibility—themes that shape *Frankenstein*. Mary saw in her own life and in the lives of others that vast damage can be done when people pursue inspiration without a corresponding respect for the feelings and the lives of others.

The story of *Frankenstein* is one of a man (Victor Frankenstein) who acts without thought for consequences and whose subsequent abandonment of his creation leaves a swath of collateral damage in its wake. Reading the novel with regard to Mary's biography, one sees in the monster the broken families, the suicides, and the lost children that represented the dark side of the Romantic movement. The story of parents failing their offspring in practical and emotional ways played out in Mary's life and the lives of her friends again and again.

The one constant of Mary's life was that parents could not be counted upon to care for or protect their children adequately. Often this happened through no fault of the parent, as when Wollstonecraft died after Mary's birth, or when Mary was unable to save her premature daughter. Other times the rejection was deliberate and blatant, as when Mary's father cut off contact with her for following the very lessons that he had taught, or when Byron refused to take any responsibility for Allegra until it became obvious to him that this was the only way to silence Claire. Sometimes the abandonment was more complicated. Percy had hoped to stay in close contact with Harriet and their children, and after she died he tried to get custody of them. However, when he had to choose between his children and Mary, he chose Mary. Even then, his choice was not constant, for whenever she was having his babies and was very pregnant or tending a newborn, he was off with someone else.

Frankenstein is a messy, melodramatic book in which characters are constantly exclaiming and swooning and missing the obvious. It's no more and no less dated than any other Romantic piece of writing. Despite that, it has lived on and part of the reason it endures is that this imaginary tale borne of a nightmare is also created from lived emotional experience.

Nineteen-year-old Mary had certainly not sewn a man together and brought him back to life, but she had dreamed of her dead baby being revived after the first Clara's death. She knew why people failed to take responsibility for their actions, especially pertaining to wives and children, and she knew how angry and desperate and vulnerable those wives and children could be.

Because of the scandal that surrounded her, she knew what it was to be feared and hated by society. At nineteen, Mary was an expert on instability, abandonment, rejection, and loss. Those emotions are what keep *Frankenstein* not just interesting, but *alive*.

ABOUT THE AUTHOR

Carrie Sessarego is the resident "geek reviewer" for *Smart Bitches, Trashy Books,* where she wrangles science fiction, fantasy romance, comics, movies, and non-fiction. Carrie's first book, *Pride, Prejudice, and Popcorn: TV and Film Adaptations of Pride and Prejudice, Wuthering Heights, and Jane Eyre,* was released in 2014. Her work has been published in *Interfictions Online, Pop Matters: After the Avengers, The WisCon Chronicles Vol. 9, Invisible 3, Clarkesworld Magazine,* and two volumes of *Speculative Fiction: The Year's Best Online Reviews, Essays and Commentary.* She spends her time wrangling her husband, daughter, dog, and three cats.

Augmentations, Assassins, and Soundtracks: A Conversation with Emily Devenport

CHRIS URIE

As we continue to receive images from exploration vehicles launched years ago from deep within our own solar system, our imaginations look farther into the black abyss of space. Once we've finished pillaging this planet, or this planet is finished with *us*, will there be another home floating out there? How will we get there when the distances between inhabitable planets are too far to hold in the mind? What will happen to people on that long journey? Will they be kind, or will they kill?

Emily Devenport tackles the "Generation Ship" sub-genre of science fiction from a whole new direction. *Medusa Uploaded* cleverly infuses this framework with sprinklings of other genres. On board two generation ships divided by class, many secrets lie waiting to be uncovered. Oichi, suspected of insurgency, is spaced out of an airlock and is discovered by one such secret. But Oichi has some secrets of her own, and some murderous ambitions to shift the balance of power.

Emily Devenport is the author of numerous novels and short stories. She was a finalist for the Philip K. Dick Award. Her latest novel *Medusa Uploaded* is available from Tor Books.

When did you know you wanted to be a writer? When did you know that you could actually do it?

I knew I wanted to be a writer by the time I was twelve. I was able to write coherently by the time I was about twenty-one, but it took another six years to teach myself how to write anything people would like to read. (Those lessons are still in progress.)

Music plays a specific and integral role in your novel. Why did you choose to include specific songs or composers?

I chose the composers and the pieces that popped into my head while I was writing the scenes. I've always loved TV and movies, and I have lived through the heyday of film composers, so I had a lot of good stuff to choose from. One of the peculiar side effects of being exposed to all of that musical drama is that I tend to imagine soundtracks for stories I'm telling. I'm not sure how much people like it, and I'm a little surprised I've gotten away with it, but I can't seem to help it.

Do you listen to music while you write? If so, what have you been listening to lately?

I have done so for other novels—but I don't currently have a good sound system (I hope to remedy that, soon). For *Medusa Uploaded* and *Medusa in the Graveyard* I visited YouTube quite a lot. Classical music and jazz are readily available there, and so are a lot of the movie/TV scores.

I have old favorites that I listen to—they're well-represented in *Medusa Uploaded*. Some other things I've been listening to lately are Mahavishnu's *Apocalypse*, an album called *Harps of the Ancient Temples*, and songs by Nick Drake.

What inspired the design of Medusa?

I think I can blame Tentacle Envy. It first began to stir in my soul when Doctor Octopus showed up in that 2004 movie, *Spider-Man 2*. I loved the prosthesis he wore, and the fact that it had an interactive AI element to it. I seriously wish I had one of those gizmos.

A Medusa Unit would be a more serious commitment. That would be a full-blown relationship, and I may be too selfish to maintain that kind of bond.

Stories that take place on generation ships are an exciting sub-genre of science fiction. Did any other authors or stories inspire you to tackle this particular kind of story?

A. E. van Vogt is the first science fiction author who immediately comes to my mind, though I'm not even sure he wrote about generation ships. I'm thinking of *Voyage of the Space Beagle*. Another possibility is Zenna Henderson, who wrote a series of short stories about aliens she called The People. They came to Earth because their sun was dying, and it took generations for them to do that.

Oddly enough, my other inspiration was Jeff Lindsay's *Dexter* series, in which a serial killer targets other serial killers. I thought that idea had interesting possibilities when applied to people on a generation ship.

What are some of the challenges of designing a generation ship?

That depends on how technical you want to get. I think the first challenge is gravity. If your people aren't living in near-earth gravity conditions, their bone density is going to change. The other physical effects of long exposure to zero-gravity conditions are still being studied. I used spin to simulate gravity on *Olympia*, though it's still an unproven theory (at least, on a scale that large). Despite the lack of test data, I prefer spin-gravity as a concept, because the idea of generating a gravitational field opens quite another can of worms. The power required would be immense. That seems like an irrational expenditure, to me.

One of the interesting things I researched was exposure to void conditions. In a lot of movies, special effects have included people's eyes blowing up, their tongues swelling, etc. I was surprised to learn that some astronauts had survived exposure to void conditions during training (and some did not). Their accounts of what happened were quite different from popular depictions. I decided that sort of death would be more merciful (and less traumatic) than drowning, because you pass out so quickly.

I didn't nail down too many specific details about *Olympia* because I wanted to preserve a sense of mystery about that setting. I did try to figure out what my parameters were concerning her technical details, and then stay inside them.

Which came first, the characters or the story concept?

The story concept came first. I used to get together with some writer buddies and shoot the breeze. We discussed the idea that a serial killer on a generation ship would be interesting, but none of us could come up with a plot and characters that jelled. That didn't happen for another twenty years, when I finally had a dream about Medusa and Oichi. I dreamed that opening sequence in Lock 212. Once I knew about them, I could start asking the questions that made the story possible.

The genesis of this story was a novelette published right here in Clarkesworld Magazine. When did you know the story was actually much larger?

I knew it before I wrote the novelette. I got halfway through "The Servant" (about 20 pages in), thinking it was a novel, and I stalled out (again). I couldn't see the way forward until I realized it could be a shorter piece. About a year after it was published in *Clarkesworld*, I began to see how the longer story should unfold.

Oichi is a fascinating character. Is there anyone or anything that inspired her?

I mentioned Dexter Morgan, from Jeff Lindsay's books. I loved how he managed to get the reader to root for a killer. I also felt enthralled with the idea of someone who could be emotionally shallow, yet also have admirable qualities. We tend to be so black-and-white in our judgments of people, and I'm fascinated with the gray areas.

Medusa Uploaded takes place in the far future, but a lot of the tech and systems feel like completely plausible extrapolations of modern day technology. Where do you see communication tech-

nology heading? Is it implants or more complex tablet computers or something entirely different?

Implants are one possibility, and I have to admit I stole the concept from Vernor Vinge. I loved the idea of being able to speak almost immediately to anyone (who is open to accept your call), and I especially loved the idea of having instant access to information. In a way, that did happen—we've got the Internet, Google, etc.

Other things drive technology besides what we want. Profit is a big consideration—sometimes it's about what they give you rather than what you want (think about CDs and LPs). I also think there would be a huge variety of tech usage based on availability and income level. I suppose young people could surprise us and decide they want nothing to do with any of that and go back to older ways of communicating and entertaining themselves. Cultural revolutions are always possible (even if they're not always desirable).

I understand there's a sequel in the works. Can you give us a little teaser?

I'm working on the edits for the sequel. I can tell you that Oichi and Medusa both get pushed out of their comfort zones, and their relationship isn't as solid as they thought it was. Some new characters show up, some old characters have surprises in store, and everyone has to improvise like crazy.

Do you have any other projects you're working on?

I've got a bunch of short stories I need to finish. I've also neglected my blog. I plan to remedy that.

ABOUT THE AUTHOR

Chris Urie is a writer and editor from Ocean City, NJ. He has written and published everything from city food guide articles to critical essays on video game level design. He currently lives in Philadelphia with an ever expanding collection of books and a small black rabbit that has an attitude problem.

Another Word:
Keeping Time
FRAN WILDE

Motion was once the enemy of time. Dust still is.

Depending on when and where it is, a clock in motion may lose increments of time in the form of water drops, humidity, sun angles or clouds, gear ticks, pendulum swings, grit, gravitational pull, and more. One of humanity's great challenges is to reduce those losses, most importantly, by creating harmonic oscillators and synchronizations.

Because keeping time is at once about marking where we are in relation to time and stopping the loss of it to the vagaries of external forces, these considerations are important, both in real time and in fiction.

When I was writing "The Synchronist" for Jonathan Strahan's last *Infinity* anthology (*Infinity's End*, July 2018), the keeping and losing of time was part of my research. In my notebook, I marked small details that have gone into holding onto the tiniest of moments since we first began to divide time into more than light and darkness. I marked points at which these moments themselves became design choices that were each then locked in time, at least for a while: the clock's "face"—humanizing the display and making it ours—the concept of "ticks," and how that's been maintained, while what's ticking—from gears to quarks—changes.

But what the disparate timepieces I encountered had most in common, from the first water clocks, to crystal and optical lattice clocks that use strontium and ytterbium atoms, to a giant clock in the desert that ticks once each year—is a struggle against loss.

Today, we're at a point in horological stability (a high-tech word for "timekeeping") where losses are judged by increments that must be measured on a quantum level. That wasn't always the case, and it may not always be so in the future. That's part of timekeeping, and clock research too—knowing what's past, what's happening now, and what should happen next.

A principle of stability in timekeeping is how precisely each clock tick matches the one that came before it and the one that will come after. It's a tiny increment of future prediction, but if we can manage to keep those tiny increments together, our grasp on the future may be better. Or at least we might think so enough to engage in better long-term planning.

This is a consideration because we're now proposing to try to map time on a scale much bigger than the circuit of a clockface. For instance, the strontium clock developed as a joint project by the National Institute of Standards and Technology and the University of Colorado and led by a physicist named Jun Ye, ticks 430 billion times per second (as determined by atomic oscillation) as opposed to Long Now Foundation's 10,000-year clock that only ticks once per year.

The planners for Long Now state that their goal is to keep time accurately for millennia. To do so, they need to create a mechanism that withstands (among other things): friction, grit, dampness, earthquakes/disaster, sabotage, and thieves. The solution was to synchronize it with the sun, power it with thermal energy, design it to tick once a year, and bury it under a mountain. The resulting clock will chime every hundred years and quixotically have a cuckoo emerge every thousand years. In this, it seems more of a symbol than a timekeeper—a message to the future from the past, rather than a means of keeping time during the present.

Large-scale timekeeping can also assist massively long-distance guidance systems where static point-based guidance (radio towers, satellites) is not yet available; it can help us more accurately map the Earth; and it can assist with planning on the scale of millennia (at least that's the guiding theory behind the the Long Now clock).

As writers, we see evidence of losses of data and time constantly while doing our research. We try to gather up some of the more interesting points.

At sea, losses of time are less common now, but once, famously, inventors raced to pioneer a way to measure time efficiently. The winner was the timepiece that lost the least amount of time in transit and was achieved by self-educated carpenter and clockmaker John Harrison after iterations of failed attempts. His H4 clock's innovative escapement reduced losses aboard ship to a matter of seconds during a transit of several months with a more efficient mechanism.

For clocks that go into space—atomic clocks—researchers including Professor Jun Ye at University of Colorado, use supercooled atoms and laser lattices to assess the passage of time. More recently, NIST physicist Andrew Ludlow's team paired two atomic clocks to eliminate even tinier losses (known as dead time), for greater precision. The new clock's nickname is the ZDT (zero dead time) clock.

What do all these clocks have to do with science fiction? In part, it is a research problem. How can we understand the scope of horological history? It is also a writing problem. How can we fit that vast history into a story about time in the far-flung future, without losing either story or tempo or the humanity of time?

Take scope, first. Even the present state of timekeeping is an enormous topic—we're at a point where one clock ticks 430 billion times, and another ticks once a year. How do you cram it all—past, present, and future possibilities, into the same timeline? (Honestly, I'm trying to do a little of that in this piece and it's ridiculous.)

Then, once you've achieved a sense of scope, with regards to history, how does that become part of the fabric of a story?

In my case, with "The Synchronist," I included historical clocks as artifacts in the story, alongside imagined clocks from other planets, and other times. I tried to acknowledge the mechanical craftsmanship of a pendulum clock along the same terms as I did a crystal lattice timepiece and a Venusian cloud clock. Doing so set a framework for the immense scope of the story and the sweep of history that ran from before the Longitude Challenge, all the way through a far-flung future.

That framework let me tell the science fictional story of a timekeeping cabal and the race to free humanity from its grasp.

Meantime, the horological artifacts that I included in the story allowed me to mark points where timekeeping has changed over time. They became the ticks of progress, representative of how we experience time, and how we manage it, as factual anchors of the story.

And in doing so, I kept coming back to one point: clocks, and stories, aren't—and cannot be—time, nor can they contain it permanently. They can represent it, they can take it up, they can quantify time, but they are only metaphors for time.

Clocks and stories are what we use to represent moments, to keep them still enough to look at, in reflections and ticks. We make them in order to limit our losses, to increase understanding, even as dust gets in the gears and our travels take us to new places.

It's very human to worry about knowing what's past, what's happening now, and what should happen next. It's human to use clocks to quantify these things. What we do with that data, and the objects that try to hold the data, is part of the story of keeping time.

ABOUT THE AUTHOR _____

Fran Wilde's novels and short stories have been nominated for two Nebula awards and a Hugo, and include her Andre Norton- and Compton-Crook-winning debut novel, *Updraft* (Tor 2015), its sequels, *Cloudbound* (2016) and *Horizon* (2017), and the novelette "The Jewel and Her Lapidary" (Tor.com Publishing 2016). Her short stories appear in *Asimov's, Tor.com, Beneath Ceaseless Skies, Shimmer, Nature,* and the 2017 Year's Best Dark Fantasy and Horror. She writes for publications including *The Washington Post, Tor.com, Clarkesworld, iO9.com,* and GeekMom.com.

Editor's Desk:
Oh, the Horror of it All!
NEIL CLARKE

Points from last month's editorial and a couple of conversations at Readercon inspired me to go on another data mining expedition. I started digging into the genre data—which the authors provide on submissions—to take a look at possible trends. The data isn't specific to themes within a genre, but that wasn't what I was after this time around. I was looking for data to indicate whether or not a specific life event—my 2012 heart attack—had caused a concrete and permanent change in my taste in fiction, and if so, should the submissions guidelines needed to be changed.

My heart attack happened in July 2012, which places it at issue 70, very close to the halfway mark in *Clarkesworld*'s history. However, in terms of stories published, that's somewhat misleading. Up through issue 60, we only published two original stories per issue. Issues 61-70 had three stories in each and starting at 95, there were four stories in every other issue. From 100 on, we've typically featured five. To further complicate things, we've more recently switched from a story count to a word count model. This change has allowed us to be a bit more flexible in publishing longer works, but has made the total number of stories per issue more variable.

As a starting point, I tossed together a quick graph to visualize my selections since 2012:

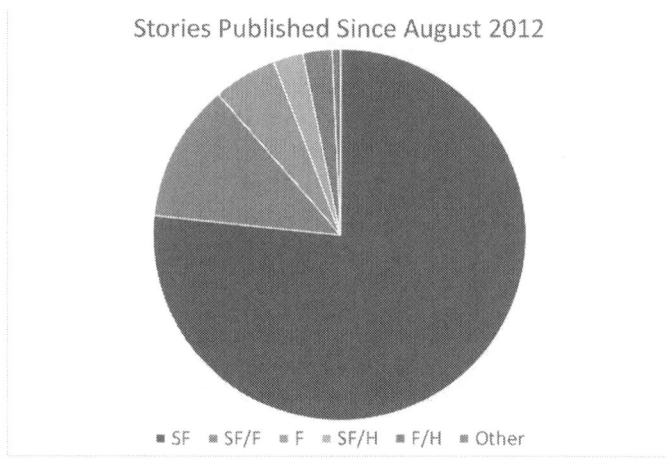

Stories Published Since August 2012

■ SF ■ SF/F ■ F ■ SF/H ■ F/H ■ Other

As you can see, approximately 77% of the stories we've published since then are categorized as science fiction by their authors and a bit more than half of what remained are science fiction/fantasy hybrids. Fantasy came in next and was followed by horror blendings with science fiction and fantasy—combined to roughly the same amount as fantasy. The tiny sliver of "other" leans much more SF than anything else (by my opinion, the authors call them a variety of subgenres). What's missing? Horror.

There's none.

And now we get to the point of my digging through the data. Since my heart attack, I've felt like there's been a disconnect with my ability to engage with that specific genre. I've had my own personal horror, and it appears to have put me off the fictional ones. I don't like to go there anymore. Yes, there are still some dark SF and dark fantasy pieces—and a lot of heavier themes—still making their way into the magazine, but it looks like I have drawn a line in the sand.

Prior to June 2012, *Clarkesworld* published some horror, but the data set is so much smaller that a single story has a much more significant impact on the percentages. I could go on about the margin of error and other things, but it would still be visually misleading—and as I've found in the past, subject to people reading their own biases into the results. There's enough armchair statisticians using bad math to score points and fuel causes. Why would I want to contribute to that?

The more I thought about it, the more I came to the realization that the "why" question I was asking myself was completely irrelevant. The history in this context doesn't matter. What matters is what I am doing now and what I intend to do in the future. There's nothing wrong with admitting that I've lost interest in the horror genre. There's no shame in feeling that way and there's nothing stopping me from changing my mind again at some later date.

It's more important that I be honest with myself, our readers, and the authors submitting their work to *Clarkesworld*. Effective today, we're changing our submissions guidelines to remove horror from the list of genres we accept. Given the last six years, that shouldn't come as a surprise to anyone, but it's time to make it official.

ABOUT THE AUTHOR

Neil Clarke is the editor of *Clarkesworld Magazine, Forever Magazine,* and *Upgraded;* owner of Wyrm Publishing; and a five-time Hugo Award Nominee for Best Editor (short form). His latest anthologies are *Galactic Empires, More Human Than Human,* and *The Final Frontier,* and the Best Science Fiction of the Year series. His next anthology, *Not One of Us.* is scheduled for publication in November 2018. He currently lives in NJ with his wife and two sons.

Cover Art: la criatura

LUIS CARLOS BARRAGÁN

Luis Carlos Barragán is a Colombian science fiction artist and writer based in Cairo, Egypt. He received his B.A in Arts in Colombia and his M.A in Islamic Art and Architecture in Egypt. His first novel, *Vagabunda Bogotá,* won the 10th award of the Cámara de Comercio de Medellin, in Colombia. His second novel, *El Gusano,* earned an honorable mention at the 2018 Isaac Asimov Awards in Puerto Real, Spain. His artwork has appeared in the indie SF magazine *Ustedes Humanos,* on the cover of the Colombian science fiction anthology *Relojes que no marcan la misma hora,* and in several issues of *Proxima Magazine,* in Argentina. He has worked as a graphic artist for Casa E, in Colombia, and the World Food Program in Egypt.

Made in the USA
Columbia, SC
10 August 2018